Jane Austen

The Novels of Jane Austen

Pride and Prejudice, Vol. 1

Jane Austen

The Novels of Jane Austen
Pride and Prejudice, Vol. 1

ISBN/EAN: 9783337208547

Printed in Europe, USA, Canada, Australia, Japan

Cover: Foto ©Andreas Hilbeck / pixelio.de

More available books at **www.hansebooks.com**

THE NOVELS OF
JANE AUSTEN

PRIDE AND PREJUDICE

VOLUME I

LONDON: GRANT RICHARDS

9 HENRIETTA STREET, W.C.

1898

PRIDE AND
PREJUDICE

I

PRIDE AND PREJUDICE

CHAPTER I

IT is a truth universally acknowledged, that a single man in possession of a good fortune must be in want of a wife.

However little known the feelings or views of such a man may be on his first entering a neighbourhood, this truth is so well fixed in the minds of the surrounding families that he is considered as the rightful property of some one or other of their daughters.

'My dear Mr. Bennet,' said his lady to him one day, 'have you heard that Netherfield Park is let at last?'

Mr. Bennet replied that he had not.

'But it is,' returned she; 'for Mrs. Long has just been here, and she told me all about it.'

Mr. Bennet made no answer.

'Do not you want to know who has taken it?' cried his wife impatiently.

'*You* want to tell me, and I have no objection to hearing it.'

This was invitation enough.

'Why, my dear, you must know, Mrs. Long says that Netherfield is taken by a young man of large fortune from the north of England ; that he came down on Monday in a chaise and four to see the place, and was so much delighted with it, that he agreed with Mr. Morris immediately ; that he is to take possession before Michaelmas, and some of his servants are to be in the house by the end of next week.'

'What is his name ?'

'Bingley.'

'Is he married or single ?'

'Oh! single, my dear, to be sure! A single man of large fortune; four or five thousand a year. What a fine thing for our girls!'

'How so? how can it affect them ?'

'My dear Mr. Bennet,' replied his wife, 'how can you be so tiresome! you must know that I am thinking of his marrying one of them.'

'Is that his design in settling here ?'

'Design! nonsense, how can you talk so! But it is very likely that he *may* fall in love with one of them, and therefore you must visit him as soon as he comes.'

'I see no occasion for that. You and the girls may go, or you may send them by themselves, which perhaps will be still better, for as you are as handsome as any of them,

Mr. Bingley might like you the best of the party.'

'My dear, you flatter me. I certainly *have* had my share of beauty, but I do not pretend to be anything extraordinary now. When a woman has five grown-up daughters she ought to give over thinking of her own beauty.'

'In such cases a woman has not often much beauty to think of.'

'But, my dear, you must indeed go and see Mr. Bingley when he comes into the neighbourhood.'

'It is more than I engage for, I assure you.'

'But consider your daughters. Only think what an establishment it would be for one of them. Sir William and Lady Lucas are determined to go, merely on that account, for in general, you know, they visit no new-comers. Indeed you must go, for it will be impossible for *us* to visit him if you do not.'

'You are over-scrupulous, surely. I dare say Mr. Bingley will be very glad to see you; and I will send a few lines by you to assure him of my hearty consent to his marrying whichever he chuses of the girls: though I must throw in a good word for my little Lizzy.'

'I desire you will do no such thing. Lizzy is not a bit better than the others; and I am sure

3

she is not half so handsome as Jane, nor half so good-humoured as Lydia. But you are always giving *her* the preference.'

'They have none of them much to recommend them,' replied he; 'they are all silly and ignorant, like other girls; but Lizzy has something more of quickness than her sisters.'

'Mr. Bennet, how can you abuse your own children in such a way! You take delight in vexing me. You have no compassion on my poor nerves.'

'You mistake me, my dear. I have a high respect for your nerves. They are my old friends. I have heard you mention them with consideration these twenty years at least.'

'Ah! you do not know what I suffer.'

'But I hope you will get over it, and live to see many young men of four thousand a year come into the neighbourhood.'

'It will be no use to us if twenty such should come, since you will not visit them.'

'Depend upon it, my dear, that when there are twenty I will visit them all.'

Mr. Bennet was so odd a mixture of quick parts, sarcastic humour, reserve, and caprice, that the experience of three-and-twenty years had been insufficient to make his wife understand his character. *Her* mind was less difficult

CHAPITRE

CHAPTER II

Mr. Bennet was among the earliest of those who waited on Mr. Bingley. He had always intended to visit him, though to the last always assuring his wife that he should not go ; and till the evening after the visit was paid she had no knowledge of it. It was then disclosed in the following manner :—Observing his second daughter employed in trimming a hat, he suddenly addressed her with—

'I hope Mr. Bingley will like it, Lizzy.'

'We are not in a way to know *what* Mr. Bingley likes,' said her mother resentfully, 'since we are not to visit.'

'But you forget, mama,' said Elizabeth, 'that we shall meet him at the assemblies, and that Mrs. Long has promised to introduce him.'

'I do not believe Mrs. Long will do any such thing. She has two nieces of her own. She is a selfish, hypocritical woman, and I have no opinion of her.'

'No more have I,' said Mr. Bennet ; 'and I

am glad to find that you do not depend on her
serving you.'

Mrs. Bennet deigned not to make any reply,
but, unable to contain herself, began scolding
one of her daughters.

'Don't keep coughing so, Kitty, for Heaven's
sake! Have a little compassion on my nerves.
You tear them to pieces.'

'Kitty has no discretion in her coughs,' said
her father; 'she times them ill.'

'I do not cough for my own amusement,' replied Kitty fretfully. 'When is your next ball
to be, Lizzy?'

'To-morrow fortnight.'

'Ay, so it is,' cried her mother; 'and Mrs.
Long does not come back till the day before;
so it will be impossible for her to introduce him,
for she will not know him herself.'

'Then, my dear, you may have the advantage
of your friend, and introduce Mr. Bingley to
her.'

'Impossible, Mr. Bennet, impossible, when I
am not acquainted with him myself; how can
you be so teasing?'

'I honour your circumspection. A fortnight's
acquaintance is certainly very little. One cannot know what a man really is by the end of a
fortnight. But if *we* do not venture somebody
else will; and after all, Mrs. Long and her

nieces must stand their chance; and, therefore, as she will think it an act of kindness, if you decline the office, I will take it on myself.'

The girls stared at their father. Mrs. Bennet said only, ' Nonsense, nonsense !'

' What can be the meaning of that emphatic exclamation ?' cried he. ' Do you consider the forms of introduction, and the stress that is laid on them, as nonsense ? I cannot quite agree with you *there.* What say you, Mary ? for you are a young lady of deep reflection, I know, and read great books and make extracts.'

Mary wished to say something very sensible, but knew not how.

' While Mary is adjusting her ideas,' he continued, ' let us return to Mr. Bingley.'

' I am sick of Mr. Bingley,' cried his wife.

' I am sorry to hear *that*; but why did not you tell me so before? If I had known as much this morning I certainly would not have called on him. It is very unlucky; but as I have actually paid the visit, we cannot escape the acquaintance now.'

The astonishment of the ladies was just what he wished; that of Mrs. Bennet perhaps surpassing the rest; though, when the first tumult of joy was over, she began to declare that it was what she had expected all the while.

' How good it was in you, my dear Mr.

Bennet! But I knew I should persuade you
at last. I was sure you loved your girls too
well to neglect such an acquaintance. Well,
how pleased I am! and it is such a good joke,
too, that you should have gone this morning
and never said a word about it till now.'

'Now, Kitty, you many cough as much as
you chuse,' said Mr. Bennet; and, as he spoke,
he left the room, fatigued with the raptures of
his wife.

'What an excellent father you have, girls!'
said she, when the door was shut. 'I do not
know how you will ever make him amends for
his kindness; or me either, for that matter. At
our time of life it is not so pleasant, I can tell
you, to be making new acquaintance every day;
but for your sakes, we would do anything.
Lydia, my love, though you *are* the youngest,
I dare say Mr. Bingley will dance with you at
the next ball.'

'Oh!' said Lydia stoutly, 'I am not afraid;
for though I *am* the youngest, I 'm the tallest.'

The rest of the evening was spent in con-
jecturing how soon he would return Mr. Bennet's
visit, and determining when they should ask him
to dinner.

CHAPTER III

NOT all that Mrs. Bennet, however, with the assistance of her five daughters, could ask on the subject, was sufficient to draw from her husband any satisfactory description of Mr. Bingley. They attacked him in various ways— with barefaced questions, ingenious suppositions, and distant surmises; but he eluded the skill of them all, and they were at last obliged to accept the second-hand intelligence of their neighbour, Lady Lucas. Her report was highly favourable. Sir William had been delighted with him. He was quite young, wonderfully handsome, extremely agreeable, and, to crown the whole, he meant to be at the next assembly with a large party. Nothing could be more delightful! To be fond of dancing was a certain step towards falling in love; and very lively hopes of Mr. Bingley's heart were entertained.

'If I can but see one of my daughters happily settled at Netherfield,' said Mrs. Bennet to her husband, 'and all the others equally well married, I shall have nothing to wish for.'

10

In a few days Mr. Bingley returned Mr. Bennet's visit, and sat about ten minutes with him in his library. He had entertained hopes of being admitted to a sight of the young ladies, of whose beauty he had heard much; but he saw only the father. The ladies were somewhat more fortunate, for they had the advantage of ascertaining from an upper window that he wore a blue coat, and rode a black horse.

An invitation to dinner was soon afterwards despatched; and already had Mrs. Bennet planned the courses that were to do credit to her house-keeping, when an answer arrived which deferred it all. Mr. Bingley was obliged to be in town the following day, and, consequently, unable to accept the honour of their invitation, etc. Mrs. Bennet was quite disconcerted. She could not imagine what business he could have in town so soon after his arrival in Hertfordshire; and she began to fear that he might always be flying about from one place to another, and never settled at Netherfield as he ought to be. Lady Lucas quieted her fears a little by starting the idea of his being gone to London only to get a large party for the ball; and a report soon followed, that Mr. Bingley was to bring twelve ladies and seven gentlemen with him to the assembly. The girls grieved over such a number of ladies, but were comforted the day before the ball by hearing that instead of twelve he had brought only six with him from London—his five sisters and a cousin. And when the party entered the assembly room it consisted of only five altogether—Mr. Bingley, his two sisters, the husband of the eldest, and another young man.

Mr. Bingley was good-looking and gentleman-like; he had a pleasant countenance, and easy, unaffected manners. His sisters were fine women, with an air of decided fashion. His brother-in-law, Mr. Hurst, merely looked the gentleman; but his friend Mr. Darcy soon drew the attention of the room by his fine, tall person, handsome features, noble mien, and the report, which was in general circulation within five minutes after his entrance, of his having ten thousand a year. The gentlemen pronounced him to be a fine figure of a man, the ladies declared he was much handsomer than Mr. Bingley, and he was looked at with great admiration for about half the evening, till his manners gave a disgust which turned the tide of his popularity; for he was discovered to be proud, to be above his company, and above being pleased; and not all his large estate in Derbyshire could then save him from having a most forbidding, disagreeable countenance, and being unworthy to be compared with his friend.

12

Mr. Bingley had soon made himself acquainted with all the principal people in the room; he was lively and unreserved, danced every dance, was angry that the ball closed so early, and talked of giving one himself at Netherfield. Such amiable qualities must speak for themselves. What a contrast between him and his friend! Mr. Darcy danced only once with Mrs. Hurst and once with Miss Bingley, declined being introduced to any other lady, and spent the rest of the evening in walking about the room, speaking occasionally to one of his own party. His character was decided. He was the proudest, most disagreeable man in the world, and everybody hoped that he would never come there again. Amongst the most violent against him was Mrs. Bennet, whose dislike of his general behaviour was sharpened into particular resentment by his having slighted one of her daughters.

Elizabeth Bennet had been obliged, by the scarcity of gentlemen, to sit down for two dances; and during part of that time Mr. Darcy had been standing near enough for her to overhear a conversation between him and Mr. Bingley, who came from the dance for a few minutes, to press his friend to join it.

'Come, Darcy,' said he, 'I must have you dance. I hate to see you standing about by yourself in this stupid manner. You had much better dance.'

'I certainly shall not. You know how I detest it, unless I am particularly acquainted with my partner. At such an assembly as this it would be insupportable. Your sisters are engaged, and there is not another woman in the room whom it would not be a punishment to me to stand up with.'

'I would not be so fastidious as you are,' cried Bingley, 'for a kingdom! Upon my honour, I never met with so many pleasant girls in my life as I have this evening; and there are several of them you see uncommonly pretty.'

'*You* are dancing with the only handsome girl in the room,' said Mr. Darcy, looking at the eldest Miss Bennet.

'Oh! she is the most beautiful creature I ever beheld! But there is one of her sisters sitting down just behind you, who is very pretty, and I dare say very agreeable. Do let me ask my partner to introduce you.'

'Which do you mean?' and turning round he looked for a moment at Elizabeth, till catching her eye, he withdrew his own and coldly said, 'She is tolerable, but not handsome enough to tempt *me*; and I am in no humour at present to give consequence to young ladies who are slighted by other men. You had better return

14

to your partner and enjoy her smiles, for you are wasting your time with me.'

Mr. Bingley followed his advice. Mr. Darcy walked off; and Elizabeth remained with no very cordial feelings towards him. She told the story, however, with great spirit among her friends; for she had a lively, playful disposition, which delighted in anything ridiculous.

The evening altogether passed off pleasantly to the whole family. Mrs. Bennet had seen her eldest daughter much admired by the Netherfield party. Mr. Bingley had danced with her twice, and she had been distinguished by his sisters. Jane was as much gratified by this as her mother could be, though in a quieter way. Elizabeth felt Jane's pleasure. Mary had heard herself mentioned to Miss Bingley as the most accomplished girl in the neighbourhood; and Catherine and Lydia had been fortunate enough to be never without partners, which was all that they had yet learnt to care for at a ball. They returned, therefore, in good spirits to Longbourn, the village where they lived, and of which they were the principal inhabitants. They found Mr. Bennet still up. With a book he was regardless of time; and on the present occasion he had a good deal of curiosity as to the event of an evening which had raised such splendid expectations. He had rather hoped that all his wife's views on the stranger would be disappointed; but he soon found that he had a very different story to hear.

'Oh! my dear Mr. Bennet,' as she entered the room, 'we have had a most delightful evening, a most excellent ball. I wish you had been there. Jane was so admired, nothing could be like it. Everybody said how well she looked; and Mr. Bingley thought her quite beautiful, and danced with her twice! Only think of *that*, my dear; he actually danced with her twice! and she was the only creature in the room that he asked a second time. First of all he asked Miss Lucas. I was so vexed to see him stand up with her! but, however, he did not admire her at all; indeed, nobody can, you know; and he seemed quite struck with Jane as she was going down the dance. So he inquired who she was, and got introduced, and asked her for the two next. Then the two third he danced with Miss King, and the two fourth with Maria Lucas, and the two fifth with Jane again, and the two sixth with Lizzy and the Boulanger.'

'If he had had any compassion for *me*,' cried her husband impatiently, 'he would not have danced half so much! For God's sake, say no more of his partners. O that he had sprained his ankle in the first dance!'

'Oh! my dear,' continued Mrs. Bennet, 'I am

quite delighted with him. He is so excessively handsome! and his sisters are charming women. I never in my life saw anything more elegant than their dresses. I dare say the lace upon Mrs. Hurst's gown——'

Here she was interrupted again. Mr. Bennet protested against any description of finery. She was therefore obliged to seek another branch of the subject, and related, with much bitterness of spirit and some exaggeration, the shocking rudeness of Mr. Darcy.

'But I can assure you,' she added, 'that Lizzy does not lose much by not suiting *his* fancy; for he is a most disagreeable, horrid man, not at all worth pleasing. So high and so conceited that there was no enduring him! He walked here, and he walked there, fancying himself so very great! Not handsome enough to dance with! I wish you had been there, my dear, to have given him one of your set-downs. I quite detest the man.'

CHAPTER IV

WHEN Jane and Elizabeth were alone, the former, who had been cautious in her praise of Mr. Bingley before, expressed to her sister how very much she admired him.

'He is just what a young man ought to be,' said she, 'sensible, good-humoured, lively; and I never saw such happy manners!—so much ease, with such perfect good-breeding!'

'He is also handsome,' replied Elizabeth; 'which a young man ought likewise to be, if he possibly can. His character is thereby complete.'

'I was very much flattered by his asking me to dance a second time. I did not expect such a compliment.'

'Did not you? *I* did for you. But that is one great difference between us. Compliments always take *you* by surprise, and *me* never. What could be more natural than his asking you again? He could not help seeing that you were about five times as pretty as every other woman in the room. No thanks to his gallantry

18

for that. Well, he certainly is very agreeable, and I give you leave to like him. You have liked many a stupider person.'

'Dear Lizzy!'

'Oh! you are a great deal too apt, you know, to like people in general. You never see a fault in anybody. All the world are good and agreeable in your eyes. I never heard you speak ill of a human being in my life.'

'I would wish not to be hasty in censuring any one; but I always speak what I think.'

'I know you do; and it is *that* which makes the wonder. With *your* good sense to be so honestly blind to the follies and nonsense of others! Affectation of candour is common enough—one meets it everywhere. But to be candid without ostentation or design—to take the good of everybody's character and make it still better, and say nothing of the bad—belongs to you alone. And so you like this man's sisters too, do you? Their manners are not equal to his.'

'Certainly not—at first. But they are very pleasing women when you converse with them. Miss Bingley is to live with her brother, and keep his house; and I am much mistaken if we shall not find a very charming neighbour in her.'

Elizabeth listened in silence, but was not convinced; their behaviour at the assembly had not

19

been calculated to please in general; and with more quickness of observation and less pliancy of temper than her sister, and with a judgment too unassailed by any attention to herself, she was very little disposed to approve them. They were in fact very fine ladies; not deficient in good-humour when they were pleased, nor in the power of being agreeable when they chose it, but proud and conceited. They were rather handsome, had been educated in one of the first private seminaries in town, had a fortune of twenty thousand pounds, were in the habit of spending more than they ought, and of associating with people of rank, and were therefore in every respect entitled to think well of themselves, and meanly of others. They were of a respectable family in the north of England; a circumstance more deeply impressed on their memories than that their brother's fortune and their own had been acquired by trade.

Mr. Bingley inherited property to the amount of nearly an hundred thousand pounds from his father, who had intended to purchase an estate, but did not live to do it. Mr. Bingley intended it likewise, and sometimes made choice of his county; but as he was now provided with a good house and the liberty of a manor, it was doubtful to many of those who best knew the easiness of his temper, whether he might not spend the remainder of his days at Netherfield and leave the next generation to purchase.

His sisters were very anxious for his having an estate of his own; but, though he was now established only as a tenant, Miss Bingley was by no means unwilling to preside at his table—nor was Mrs. Hurst, who had married a man of more fashion than fortune, less disposed to consider his house as her home when it suited her. Mr. Bingley had not been of age two years when he was tempted by an accidental recommendation to look at Netherfield House. He did look at it, and into it, for half an hour—was pleased with the situation and the principal rooms, satisfied with what the owner said in its praise, and took it immediately.

Between him and Darcy there was a very steady friendship, in spite of great opposition of character. Bingley was endeared to Darcy by the easiness, openness, and ductility of his temper, though no disposition could offer a greater contrast to his own, and though with his own he never appeared dissatisfied. On the strength of Darcy's regard Bingley had the firmest reliance, and of his judgment the highest opinion. In understanding, Darcy was the superior. Bingley was by no means deficient, but Darcy was clever. He was at the same time haughty, reserved, and fastidious, and his manners, though well-bred, were not inviting. In that respect his friend had greatly the advantage. Bingley was sure of being liked wherever he appeared, Darcy was continually giving offence.

The manner in which they spoke of the Meryton assembly was sufficiently characteristic. Bingley had never met with pleasanter people or prettier girls in his life; everybody had been most kind and attentive to him; there had been no formality, no stiffness; he had soon felt acquainted with all the room; and as to Miss Bennet, he could not conceive an angel more beautiful. Darcy, on the contrary, had seen a collection of people in whom there was little beauty and no fashion, for none of whom he had felt the smallest interest, and from none received either attention or pleasure. Miss Bennet he acknowledged to be pretty, but she smiled too much.

Mrs. Hurst and her sister allowed it to be so; but still they admired her and liked her, and pronounced her to be a sweet girl, and one whom they should not object to know more of. Miss Bennet was therefore established as a sweet girl, and their brother felt authorised by such commendation to think of her as he chose.

CHAPTER V

WITHIN a short walk of Longbourn lived a family with whom the Bennets were particularly intimate. Sir William Lucas had been formerly in trade in Meryton, where he had made a tolerable fortune, and risen to the honour of knighthood by an address to the king, during his mayoralty. The distinction had perhaps been felt too strongly. It had given him a disgust to his business, and to his residence in a small market town ; and, quitting them both, he had removed with his family to an house about a mile from Meryton, denominated from that period Lucas Lodge, where he could think with pleasure of his own importance, and, unshackled by business, occupy himself solely in being civil to all the world. For, though elated by his rank, it did not render him supercilious ; on the contrary, he was all attention to everybody. By nature inoffensive, friendly, and obliging, his presentation at St. James's had made him courteous.

Lady Lucas was a very good kind of woman,

PRIDE AND PREJUDICE

not too clever to be a valuable neighbour to
Mrs. Bennet. They had several children. The
eldest of them, a sensible, intelligent young
woman, about twenty-seven, was Elizabeth's
intimate friend.

That the Miss Lucases and the Miss Bennets
should meet to talk over a ball was absolutely
necessary; and the morning after the assembly
brought the former to Longbourn to hear and
to communicate.

'*You* began the evening well, Charlotte,' said
Mrs. Bennet, with civil self-command, to Miss
Lucas. '*You* were Mr. Bingley's first choice.'

'Yes; but he seemed to like his second
better.'

'Oh! you mean Jane, I suppose, because he
danced with her twice. To be sure that *did*
seem as if he admired her—indeed I rather
believe he *did*—I heard something about it—
but I hardly know what—something about Mr.
Robinson.'

'Perhaps you mean what I overheard between
him and Mr. Robinson: did not I mention it
to you? Mr. Robinson's asking him how he
liked our Meryton assemblies, and whether he
did not think there were a great many pretty
women in the room, and *which* he thought the
prettiest? and his answering immediately to
the last question—" Oh! the eldest Miss Bennet,

beyond a doubt; there cannot be two opinions on that point."'

'Upon my word! Well, that was very decided indeed—that does seem as if——but, however, it may all come to nothing, you know.'

'*My* overhearings were more to the purpose than *yours*, Eliza,' said Charlotte. 'Mr. Darcy is not so well worth listening to as his friend, is he? Poor Eliza! to be only just *tolerable*.'

'I beg you would not put it into Lizzy's head to be vexed by his ill-treatment, for he is such a disagreeable man, that it would be quite a misfortune to be liked by him. Mrs. Long told me last night that he sat close to her for half an hour without once opening his lips.'

'Are you quite sure, ma'am? is not there a little mistake?' said Jane. 'I certainly saw Mr. Darcy speaking to her.'

'Ay—because she asked him at last how he liked Netherfield, and he could not help answering her; but she said he seemed very angry at being spoke to.'

'Miss Bingley told me,' said Jane, 'that he never speaks much, unless among his intimate acquaintance. With *them* he is remarkably agreeable.'

'I do not believe a word of it, my dear. If he had been so very agreeable, he would have talked to Mrs. Long. But I can guess how it

25

was : everybody says that he is eat up with pride, and I dare say he had heard somehow that Mrs. Long does not keep a carriage, and had come to the ball in a hack chaise.'

'I do not mind his not talking to Mrs. Long,' said Miss Lucas, 'but I wish he had danced with Eliza.'

'Another time, Lizzy,' said her mother, 'I would not dance with *him*, if I were you.'

'I believe, ma'am, I may safely promise you *never* to dance with him.'

'His pride,' said Miss Lucas, 'does not offend *me* so much as pride often does, because there is an excuse for it. One cannot wonder that so very fine a young man, with family, fortune, everything in his favour, should think highly of himself. If I may so express it, he has a *right* to be proud.'

'That is very true,' replied Elizabeth, 'and I could easily forgive *his* pride, if he had not mortified *mine*.'

'Pride,' observed Mary, who piqued herself upon the solidity of her reflections, 'is a very common failing, I believe. By all that I have ever read, I am convinced that it is very common indeed ; that human nature is particularly prone to it, and that there are very few of us who do not cherish a feeling of self-complacency on the score of some quality or other, real or imaginary.

26

Vanity and pride are different things, though the words are often used synonymously. A person may be proud without being vain. Pride relates more to our opinion of ourselves, vanity to what we would have others think of us.'

'If I were as rich as Mr. Darcy,' cried a young Lucas, who came with his sisters, 'I should not care how proud I was. I would keep a pack of foxhounds, and drink a bottle of wine every day.'

'Then you would drink a great deal more than you ought,' said Mrs. Bennet; 'and if I were to see you at it, I should take away your bottle directly.'

The boy protested that she should not; she continued to declare that she would, and the argument ended only with the visit.

CHAPTER VI

THE ladies of Longbourn soon waited on those of Netherfield. The visit was returned in due form. Miss Bennet's pleasing manners grew on the goodwill of Mrs. Hurst and Miss Bingley; and though the mother was found to be intolerable, and the younger sisters not worth speaking to, a wish of being better acquainted with *them* was expressed towards the two eldest. By Jane, this attention was received with the greatest pleasure; but Elizabeth still saw superciliousness in their treatment of everybody, hardly excepting even her sister, and could not like them; though their kindness to Jane, such as it was, had a value as arising in all probability from the influence of their brother's admiration. It was generally evident whenever they met, that he *did* admire her; and to *her* it was equally evident that Jane was yielding to the preference which she had begun to entertain for him from the first, and was in a way to be very much in love; but she considered with pleasure that it was not likely to be discovered by the

world in general, since Jane united, with great
strength of feeling, a composure of temper and
a uniform cheerfulness of manner which would
guard her from the suspicions of the impertinent.
She mentioned this to her friend Miss Lucas.

'It may perhaps be pleasant,' replied Charlotte,
'to be able to impose on the public in such
a case; but it is sometimes a disadvantage to
be so very guarded. If a woman conceals her
affection with the same skill from the object of
it, she may lose the opportunity of fixing him;
and it will then be but poor consolation to
believe the world equally in the dark. There is
so much of gratitude or vanity in almost every
attachment, that it is not safe to leave any to
itself. We can all *begin* freely—a slight preference is natural enough; but there are very few
of us who have heart enough to be really in love
without encouragement. In nine cases out of
ten a woman had better show *more* affection
than she feels. Bingley likes your sister undoubtedly; but he may never do more than like
her, if she does not help him on.'

'But she does help him on, as much as her
nature will allow. If *I* can perceive her regard
for him, he must be a simpleton, indeed, not to
discover it too.'

'Remember, Eliza, that he does not know
Jane's disposition as you do.'

'But if a woman is partial to a man, and does not endeavour to conceal it, he must find it out.'

'Perhaps he must, if he sees enough of her. But, though Bingley and Jane meet tolerably often, it is never for many hours together; and as they always see each other in large mixed parties, it is impossible that every moment should be employed in conversing together. Jane should therefore make the most of every half-hour in which she can command his attention. When she is secure of him, there will be leisure for falling in love as much as she chuses.'

'Your plan is a good one,' replied Elizabeth, 'where nothing is in question but the desire of being well married; and if I were determined to get a rich husband, or any husband, I dare say I should adopt it. But these are not Jane's feelings; she is not acting by design. As yet, she cannot even be certain of the degree of her own regard, nor of its reasonableness. She has known him only a fortnight. She danced four dances with him at Meryton; she saw him one morning at his own house, and has since dined in company with him four times. This is not quite enough to make her understand his character.'

'Not as you represent it. Had she merely *dined* with him, she might only have discovered whether he had a good appetite; but you must remember that four evenings have been also spent together—and four evenings may do a great deal.'

'Yes; these four evenings have enabled them to ascertain that they both like Vingt-un better than Commerce; but with respect to any other leading characteristic, I do not imagine that much has been unfolded.'

'Well,' said Charlotte, 'I wish Jane success with all my heart; and if she were married to him to-morrow, I should think she had as good a chance of happiness as if she were to be studying his character for a twelvemonth. Happiness in marriage is entirely a matter of chance. If the dispositions of the parties are ever so well known to each other, or ever so similar beforehand, it does not advance their felicity in the least. They always continue to grow sufficiently unlike afterwards to have their share of vexation; and it is better to know as little as possible of the defects of the person with whom you are to pass your life.'

'You make me laugh, Charlotte; but it is not sound. You know it is not sound, and that you would never act in this way yourself.'

Occupied in observing Mr. Bingley's attentions to her sister, Elizabeth was far from suspecting that she was herself becoming an object of some interest in the eyes of his friend. Mr. Darcy

had at first scarcely allowed her to be pretty : he
had looked at her without admiration at the
ball; and when they next met, he looked at her
only to criticise. But no sooner had he made it
clear to himself and his friends that she had
hardly a good feature in her face, than he began
to find it was rendered uncommonly intelligent
by the beautiful expression of her dark eyes.
To this discovery succeeded some others equally
mortifying. Though he had detected with a
critical eye more than one failure of perfect
symmetry in her form, he was forced to acknowledge her figure to be light and pleasing; and in
spite of his asserting that her manners were not
those of the fashionable world, he was caught by
their easy playfulness. Of this she was perfectly
unaware ;—to her he was only the man who
made himself agreeable nowhere, and who had
not thought her handsome enough to dance with.

He began to wish to know more of her, and
as a step towards conversing with her himself,
attended to her conversation with others. His
doing so drew her notice. It was at Sir William
Lucas's, where a large party were assembled.

'What does Mr. Darcy mean,' said she to
Charlotte, 'by listening to my conversation with
Colonel Forster?'

'That is a question which Mr. Darcy only can
answer.'

'But if he does it any more I shall certainly let him know that I see what he is about. He has a very satirical eye, and if I do not begin by being impertinent myself, I shall soon grow afraid of him.'

On his approaching them soon afterwards, though without seeming to have any intention of speaking, Miss Lucas defied her friend to mention such a subject to him; which immediately provoking Elizabeth to do it, she turned to him and said—

'Did not you think, Mr. Darcy, that I expressed myself uncommonly well just now, when I was teasing Colonel Forster to give us a ball at Meryton?'

'With great energy; but it is a subject which always makes a lady energetic.'

'You are severe on us.'

'It will be *her* turn soon to be teased,' said Miss Lucas. 'I am going to open the instrument, Eliza, and you know what follows.'

'You are a very strange creature by way of a friend!—always wanting me to play and sing before anybody and everybody! If my vanity had taken a musical turn, you would have been invaluable; but as it is, I would really rather not sit down before those who must be in the habit of hearing the very best performers.' On Miss Lucas's persevering, however, she added,

'Very well; if it must be so, it must.' And gravely glancing at Mr. Darcy, 'There is a fine old saying, which everybody here is of course familiar with—"Keep your breath to cool your porridge"—and I shall keep mine to swell my song.'

Her performance was pleasing, though by no means capital. After a song or two, and before she could reply to the entreaties of several that she would sing again, she was eagerly succeeded at the instrument by her sister Mary, who having, in consequence of being the only plain one in the family, worked hard for knowledge and accomplishments, was always impatient for display.

Mary had neither genius nor taste; and though vanity had given her application, it had given her likewise a pedantic air and conceited manner, which would have injured a higher degree of excellence than she had reached. Elizabeth, easy and unaffected, had been listened to with much more pleasure, though not playing half so well; and Mary, at the end of a long concerto, was glad to purchase praise and gratitude by Scotch and Irish airs, at the request of her younger sisters, who, with some of the Lucases, and two or three officers, joined eagerly in dancing at one end of the room.

Mr. Darcy stood near them in silent indignation at such a mode of passing the evening, to the exclusion of all conversation, and was too much engrossed by his thoughts to perceive that Sir William Lucas was his neighbour, till Sir William thus began—

'What a charming amusement for young people this is, Mr. Darcy! There is nothing like dancing after all. I consider it as one of the first refinements of polished societies.'

'Certainly, sir; and it has the advantage also of being in vogue amongst the less polished societies of the world. Every savage can dance.'

Sir William only smiled. 'Your friend performs delightfully,' he continued after a pause, on seeing Bingley join the group; 'and I doubt not that you are an adept in the science yourself, Mr. Darcy.'

'You saw me dance at Meryton, I believe, sir.'

'Yes, indeed, and received no inconsiderable pleasure from the sight. Do you often dance at St. James's?'

'Never, sir.'

'Do you not think it would be a proper compliment to the place?'

'It is a compliment which I never pay to any place if I can avoid it.'

'You have a house in town, I conclude?'

Mr. Darcy bowed.

'I had once some thoughts of fixing in town myself—for I am fond of superior society; but I did not feel quite certain that the air of London would agree with Lady Lucas.'

He paused in hopes of an answer; but his companion was not disposed to make any; and Elizabeth at that instant moving towards them, he was struck with the notion of doing a very gallant thing, and called out to her—

'My dear Miss Eliza, why are not you dancing?—Mr. Darcy, you must allow me to present this young lady to you as a very desirable partner. You cannot refuse to dance, I am sure, when so much beauty is before you.' And, taking her hand, he would have given it to Mr. Darcy, who, though extremely surprised, was not unwilling to receive it, when she instantly drew back, and said with some discomposure to Sir William—

'Indeed, sir, I have not the least intention of dancing. I entreat you not to suppose that I moved this way in order to beg for a partner.'

Mr. Darcy, with grave propriety, requested to be allowed the honour of her hand, but in vain. Elizabeth was determined; nor did Sir William at all shake her purpose by his attempt at persuasion.

'You excel so much in the dance, Miss Eliza, that it is cruel to deny me the happiness of seeing you; and though this gentleman dislikes the amusement in general, he can have no objection, I am sure, to oblige us for one half-hour.'

'Mr. Darcy is all politeness,' said Elizabeth, smiling.

'He is indeed; but considering the induce-ment, my dear Miss Eliza, we cannot wonder at his complaisance—for who would object to such a partner?'

Elizabeth looked archly, and turned away. Her resistance had not injured her with the gentleman, and he was thinking of her with some compla-cency, when thus accosted by Miss Bingley—

'I can guess the subject of your reverie.'

'I should imagine not.'

'You are considering how insupportable it would be to pass many evenings in this manner —in such society; and indeed I am quite of your opinion. I was never more annoyed! The insipidity, and yet the noise—the nothingness, and yet the self-importance of all these people! What would I give to hear your strictures on them!'

'Your conjecture is totally wrong, I assure you. My mind was more agreeably engaged. I have been meditating on the very great pleasure which a pair of fine eyes in the face of a pretty woman can bestow.'

3 c*   37

Miss Bingley immediately fixed her eyes on his face, and desired he would tell her what lady had the credit of inspiring such reflections. Mr. Darcy replied with great intrepidity—

'Miss Elizabeth Bennet.'

'Miss Elizabeth Bennet!' repeated Miss Bingley. 'I am all astonishment. How long has she been such a favourite?—and pray, when am I to wish you joy?'

'That is exactly the question which I expected you to ask. A lady's imagination is very rapid: it jumps from admiration to love, from love to matrimony, in a moment. I knew you would be wishing me joy.'

'Nay, if you are so serious about it, I shall consider the matter as absolutely settled. You will have a charming mother-in-law, indeed; and, of course, she will be always at Pemberley with you.'

He listened to her with perfect indifference while she chose to entertain herself in this manner; and as his composure convinced her that all was safe, her wit flowed long.

CHAPTER VII

MR. BENNET'S property consisted almost entirely in an estate of two thousand a year, which, unfortunately for his daughters, was entailed, in default of heirs-male, on a distant relation; and their mother's fortune, though ample for her situation in life, could but ill supply the deficiency of his. Her father had been an attorney in Meryton, and had left her four thousand pounds.

She had a sister married to a Mr. Philips, who had been a clerk to their father, and succeeded him in the business, and a brother settled in London in a respectable line of trade.

The village of Longbourn was only one mile from Meryton; a most convenient distance for the young ladies, who were usually tempted thither three or four times a week, to pay their duty to their aunt and to a milliner's shop just over the way. The two youngest of the family, Catherine and Lydia, were particularly frequent in these attentions; their minds were more vacant than their sisters', and when nothing

better offered, a walk to Meryton was necessary
to amuse their morning hours and furnish conversation for the evening; and however bare
of news the country in general might be, they
always contrived to learn some from their aunt.
At present, indeed, they were well supplied both
with news and happiness by the recent arrival of
a militia regiment in the neighbourhood; it was
to remain the whole winter, and Meryton was
the headquarters.

Their visits to Mrs. Philips were now produc-
tive of the most interesting intelligence. Every
day added something to their knowledge of the
officers' names and connexions. Their lodgings
were not long a secret, and at length they began
to know the officers themselves. Mr. Philips
visited them all, and this opened to his nieces a
source of felicity unknown before. They could
talk of nothing but officers; and Mr. Bingley's
large fortune, the mention of which gave animation to their mother, was worthless in their
eyes when opposed to the regimentals of an
ensign.

After listening one morning to their effusions.
on this subject, Mr. Bennet coolly observed—

'From all that I can collect by your manner
of talking, you must be two of the silliest girls
in the country. I have suspected it some time,
but I am now convinced.'

40

Catherine was disconcerted, and made no answer; but Lydia, with perfect indifference, continued to express her admiration of Captain Carter, and her hope of seeing him in the course of the day, as he was going the next morning to London.

'I am astonished, my dear,' said Mrs. Bennet, 'that you should be so ready to think your own children silly. If I wished to think slightingly of anybody's children, it should not be of my own, however.'

'If my children are silly, I must hope to be always sensible of it.'

'Yes—but as it happens, they are all of them very clever.'

'This is the only point, I flatter myself, on which we do not agree. I had hoped that our sentiments coincided in every particular, but I must so far differ from you as to think our two youngest daughters uncommonly foolish.'

'My dear Mr. Bennet, you must not expect such girls to have the sense of their father and mother. When they get to our age I dare say they will not think about officers any more than we do. I remember the time when I liked a red coat myself very well—and, indeed, so I do still at my heart; and if a smart young colonel, with five or six thousand a year, should want one of my girls, I shall not say nay to him; and

41

I thought Colonel Forster looked very becoming the other night at Sir William's in his regimentals.'

'Mama,' cried Lydia, 'my aunt says that Colonel Forster and Captain Carter do not go so often to Miss Watson's as they did when they first came; she sees them now very often standing in Clarke's library.'

Mrs. Bennet was prevented replying by the entrance of the footman with a note for Miss Bennet; it came from Netherfield, and the servant waited for an answer. Mrs. Bennet's eyes sparkled with pleasure, and she was eagerly calling out, while her daughter read—

'Well, Jane, who is it from? what is it about? what does he say? Well, Jane, make haste and tell us; make haste, my love.'

'It is from Miss Bingley,' said Jane, and then read it aloud.

'MY DEAR FRIEND,—If you are not so compassionate as to dine to-day with Louisa and me, we shall be in danger of hating each other for the rest of our lives, for a whole day's *tête-à-tête* between two women can never end without a quarrel. Come as soon as you can on the receipt of this. My brother and the gentlemen are to dine with the officers.—Yours ever,

'CAROLINE BINGLEY.'

' With the officers!' cried Lydia. 'I wonder my aunt did not tell us of *that*.'

' Dining out,' said Mrs. Bennet; 'that is very unlucky.'

' Can I have the carriage?' said Jane.

' No, my dear, you had better go on horseback, because it seems likely to rain; and then you must stay all night.'

' That would be a good scheme,' said Elizabeth, ' if you were sure that they would not offer to send her home.'

' Oh! but the gentlemen will have Mr. Bingley's chaise to go to Meryton; and the Hursts have no horses to theirs.'

' I had much rather go in the coach.'

' But, my dear, your father cannot spare the horses, I am sure. They are wanted in the farm, Mr. Bennet, are not they?'

' They are wanted in the farm much oftener than I can get them.'

' But if you have got them to-day,' said Elizabeth, ' my mother's purpose will be answered.'

She did at last extort from her father an acknowledgment that the horses were engaged: Jane was therefore obliged to go on horseback, and her mother attended her to the door with many cheerful prognostics of a bad day. Her hopes were answered: Jane had not been

43

gone long before it rained hard. Her sisters were uneasy for her, but her mother was delighted. The rain continued the whole evening without intermission : Jane certainly could not come back.

'This was a lucky idea of mine, indeed!' said Mrs. Bennet more than once, as if the credit of making it rain were all her own. Till the next morning, however, she was not aware of all the felicity of her contrivance. Breakfast was scarcely over when a servant from Netherfield brought the following note for Elizabeth—

'MY DEAREST LIZZY, — I find myself very unwell this morning, which, I suppose, is to be imputed to my getting wet through yesterday. My kind friends will not hear of my returning home till I am better. They insist also on my seeing Mr. Jones—therefore do not be alarmed if you should hear of his having been to me— and, excepting a sore throat and headache, there is not much the matter with me.—Yours, etc.'

'Well, my dear,' said Mr. Bennet, when Elizabeth had read the note aloud, 'if your daughter should have a dangerous fit of illness —if she should die, it would be a comfort to know that it was all in pursuit of Mr. Bingley, and under your orders.'

'Oh! I am not at all afraid of her dying.
People do not die of little trifling colds. She
will be taken good care of. As long as she
stays there, it is all very well. I would go and
see her if I could have the carriage.'

Elizabeth, feeling really anxious, was determined to go to her, though the carriage was not
to be had; and as she was no horsewoman,
walking was her only alternative. She declared
her resolution.

'How can you be so silly,' cried her mother,
'as to think of such a thing, in all this dirt!
You will not be fit to be seen when you get
there.'

'I shall be very fit to see Jane—which is all
I want.'

'Is this a hint to me, Lizzy,' said her father,
'to send for the horses?'

'No, indeed. I do not wish to avoid the
walk. The distance is nothing when one has
a motive; only three miles. I shall be back by
dinner.'

'I admire the activity of your benevolence,'
observed Mary, 'but every impulse of feeling
should be guided by reason; and, in my opinion,
exertion should always be in proportion to what
is required.'

'We will go as far as Meryton with you,'
said Catherine and Lydia. Elizabeth accepted

their company, and the three young ladies set off together.

'If we make haste,' said Lydia, as they walked along, 'perhaps we may see something of Captain Carter before he goes.'

In Meryton they parted; the two youngest repaired to the lodgings of one of the officer's wives, and Elizabeth continued her walk alone, crossing field after field at a quick pace, jumping over stiles and springing over puddles with impatient activity, and finding herself at last within view of the house, with weary ankles, dirty stockings, and a face glowing with the warmth of exercise.

She was shewn into the breakfast-parlour, where all but Jane were assembled, and where her appearance created a great deal of surprise. That she should have walked three miles so early in the day, in such dirty weather, and by herself, was almost incredible to Mrs. Hurst and Miss Bingley; and Elizabeth was convinced that they held her in contempt for it. She was received, however, very politely by them; and in their brother's manners there was something better than politeness; there was good-humour and kindness. Mr. Darcy said very little, and Mr. Hurst nothing at all. The former was divided between admiration of the brilliancy which exercise had given to her complexion, and doubt as to the occasion's justifying her coming so far alone. The latter was thinking only of his breakfast.

Her inquiries after her sister were not very favourably answered. Miss Bennet had slept ill, and though up, was very feverish, and not well enough to leave her room. Elizabeth was glad to be taken to her immediately; and Jane, who had only been withheld by the fear of giving alarm or inconvenience from expressing in her note how much she longed for such a visit, was delighted at her entrance. She was not equal, however, to much conversation, and when Miss Bingley left them together, could attempt little beside expressions of gratitude for the extraordinary kindness she was treated with. Elizabeth silently attended her.

When breakfast was over they were joined by the sisters; and Elizabeth began to like them herself, when she saw how much affection and solicitude they shewed for Jane. The apothecary came, and having examined his patient, said, as might be supposed, that she had caught a violent cold, and that they must endeavour to get the better of it; advised her to return to bed, and promised her some draughts. The advice was followed readily, for the feverish symptoms increased, and her head ached acutely. Elizabeth did not quit her room for a moment, nor were the other ladies often absent : the gentlemen being out, they had, in fact, nothing to do elsewhere.

When the clock struck three Elizabeth felt that she must go, and very unwillingly said so. Miss Bingley offered her the carriage, and she only wanted a little pressing to accept it, when Jane testified such concern in parting with her, that Miss Bingley was obliged to convert the offer of the chaise into an invitation to remain at Netherfield for the present. Elizabeth most thankfully consented, and a servant was despatched to Longbourn to acquaint the family with her stay and bring back a supply of clothes.

CHAPTER VIII

At five o'clock the two ladies retired to dress, and at half-past six Elizabeth was summoned to dinner. To the civil inquiries which then poured in, and amongst which she had the pleasure of distinguishing the much superior solicitude of Mr. Bingley's, she could not make a very favourable answer. Jane was by no means better. The sisters, on hearing this, repeated three or four times how much they were grieved, how shocking it was to have a bad cold, and how excessively they disliked being ill themselves; and then thought no more of the matter; and their indifference towards Jane when not immediately before them restored Elizabeth to the enjoyment of all her original dislike.

Their brother, indeed, was the only one of the party whom she could regard with any complacency. His anxiety for Jane was evident, and his attentions to herself most pleasing, and they prevented her feeling herself so much an intruder as she believed she was considered by the others. She had very little notice from any

but him. Miss Bingley was engrossed by Mr.
Darcy, her sister scarcely less so; and as for
Mr. Hurst, by whom Elizabeth sat, he was an
indolent man, who lived only to eat, drink, and
play at cards; who, when he found her prefer
a plain dish to a ragout, had nothing to say
to her.

When dinner was over she returned directly
to Jane, and Miss Bingley began abusing her as
soon as she was out of the room. Her manners
were pronounced to be very bad indeed, a mixture of pride and impertinence; she had no
conversation, no style, no taste, no beauty. Mrs.
Hurst thought the same, and added—

'She has nothing, in short, to recommend her,
but being an excellent walker. I shall never
forget her appearance this morning. She really
looked almost wild.'

'She did indeed, Louisa. I could hardly
keep my countenance. Very nonsensical to
come at all! Why must *she* be scampering
about the country, because her sister had a cold?
Her hair, so untidy, so blowsy!'

'Yes, and her petticoat; I hope you saw her
petticoat, six inches deep in mud, I am absolutely certain; and the gown which had been
let down to hide it not doing its office.'

'Your picture may be very exact, Louisa,'
said Bingley; 'but this was all lost upon me.

I thought Miss Elizabeth Bennet looked remarkably well when she came into the room this
morning. Her dirty petticoat quite escaped my
notice.'

'*You* observed it, Mr. Darcy, I am sure,' said
Miss Bingley; 'and I am inclined to think that
you would not wish to see *your sister* make such
an exhibition.'

'Certainly not.'

'To walk three miles, or four miles, or five
miles, or whatever it is, above her ankles in dirt,
and alone, quite alone! what could she mean
by it? It seems to me to shew an abominable
sort of conceited independence, a most country-
town indifference to decorum.'

'It shews an affection for her sister that is
very pleasing,' said Bingley.

'I am afraid, Mr. Darcy,' observed Miss
Bingley, in a half-whisper, 'that this adventure
has rather affected your admiration of her fine
eyes.'

'Not at all,' he replied; 'they were brightened
by the exercise.' A short pause followed this
speech, and Mrs. Hurst began again—

'I have an excessive regard for Jane Bennet;
she is really a very sweet girl, and I wish with
all my heart she were well settled. But with
such a father and mother, and such low connexions, I am afraid there is no chance of it.'

'I think I have heard you say that their uncle is an attorney in Meryton.'

'Yes; and they have another, who lives somewhere near Cheapside.'

'That is capital,' added her sister, and they both laughed heartily.

'If they had uncles enough to fill *all* Cheapside,' cried Bingley, 'it would not make them one jot less agreeable.'

'But it must very materially lessen their chance of marrying men of any consideration in the world,' replied Darcy.

To this speech Bingley made no answer; but his sisters gave it their hearty assent, and indulged their mirth for some time at the expense of their dear friend's vulgar relations.

With a renewal of tenderness, however, they repaired to her room on leaving the dining-parlour, and sat with her till summoned to coffee. She was still very poorly, and Elizabeth would not quit her at all, till late in the evening, when she had the comfort of seeing her asleep, and when it appeared to her rather right than pleasant that she should go downstairs herself. On entering the drawing-room she found the whole party at loo, and was immediately invited to join them; but suspecting them to be playing high, she declined it, and making her sister the excuse, said she would amuse herself, for the short time she could stay below, with a book. Mr. Hurst looked at her with astonishment.

'Do you prefer reading to cards?' said he; 'that is rather singular.'

'Miss Eliza Bennet,' said Miss Bingley, 'despises cards. She is a great reader, and has no pleasure in anything else.'

'I deserve neither such praise nor such censure,' cried Elizabeth; 'I am *not* a great reader, and I have pleasure in many things.'

'In nursing your sister I am sure you have pleasure,' said Bingley; 'and I hope it will soon be increased by seeing her quite well.'

Elizabeth thanked him from her heart, and then walked towards a table where a few books were lying. He immediately offered to fetch her others—all that his library afforded.

'And I wish my collection were larger for your benefit and my own credit; but I am an idle fellow, and though I have not many, I have more than I ever look into.'

Elizabeth assured him that she could suit herself perfectly with those in the room.

'I am astonished,' said Miss Bingley, 'that my father should have left so small a collection of books. What a delightful library you have at Pemberley, Mr. Darcy!'

'It ought to be good,' he replied; 'it has been the work of many generations.'

'And then you have added so much to it yourself; you are always buying books.'

'I cannot comprehend the neglect of a family library in such days as these.'

'Neglect! I am sure you neglect nothing that can add to the beauties of that noble place. Charles, when you build *your* house, I wish it may be half as delightful as Pemberley.'

'I wish it may.'

'But I would really advise you to make your purchase in that neighbourhood, and take Pemberley for a kind of model. There is not a finer county in England than Derbyshire.'

'With all my heart; I will buy Pemberley itself if Darcy will sell it.'

'I am talking of possibilities, Charles.'

'Upon my word, Caroline, I should think it more possible to get Pemberley by purchase than by imitation.'

Elizabeth was so much caught by what passed as to leave her very little attention for her book; and soon laying it wholly aside, she drew near the card-table, and stationed herself between Mr. Bingley and his eldest sister, to observe the game.

'Is Miss Darcy much grown since the spring?' said Miss Bingley; 'will she be as tall as I am?'

'I think she will. She is now about Miss Elizabeth Bennet's height, or rather taller.'

'How I long to see her again! I never met with anybody who delighted me so much. Such a countenance, such manners! and so extremely accomplished for her age! Her performance on the pianoforte is exquisite.'

'It is amazing to me,' said Bingley, 'how young ladies can have patience to be so very accomplished as they all are.'

'All young ladies accomplished! My dear Charles, what do you mean?'

'Yes, all of them, I think. They all paint tables, cover screens, and net purses. I scarcely know any one who cannot do all this, and I am sure I never heard a young lady spoken of for the first time, without being informed that she was very accomplished.'

'Your list of the common extent of accomplishments,' said Darcy, 'has too much truth. The word is applied to many a woman who deserves it no otherwise than by netting a purse or covering a screen. But I am very far from agreeing with you in your estimation of ladies in general. I cannot boast of knowing more than half a dozen, in the whole range of my acquaintance, that are really accomplished.'

'Nor I, I am sure,' said Miss Bingley.

''Then,' observed Elizabeth, 'you must comprehend a great deal in your idea of an accomplished woman.'

'Yes, I do comprehend a great deal in it.'

'Oh! certainly,' cried his faithful assistant, 'no one can be really esteemed accomplished who does not greatly surpass what is usually met with. A woman must have a thorough knowledge of music, singing, drawing, dancing, and the modern languages, to deserve the word; and besides all this, she must possess a certain something in her air and manner of walking, the tone of her voice, her address and expressions, or the word will be but half deserved.'

'All this she must possess,' added Darcy, 'and to all this she must yet add something more substantial, in the improvement of her mind by extensive reading.'

'I am no longer surprised at your knowing *only* six accomplished women. I rather wonder now at your knowing *any*.'

'Are you so severe upon your own sex as to doubt the possibility of all this?'

'*I* never saw such a woman. *I* never saw such capacity, and taste, and application, and elegance, as you describe united.'

Mrs. Hurst and Miss Bingley both cried out against the injustice of her implied doubt, and were both protesting that they knew many women who answered this description, when

Mr. Hurst called them to order, with bitter complaints of their inattention to what was going forward. As all conversation was thereby at an end, Elizabeth soon afterwards left the room.

'Eliza Bennet,' said Miss Bingley, when the door was closed on her, 'is one of those young ladies who seek to recommend themselves to the other sex by undervaluing their own; and with many men, I dare say, it succeeds. But, in my opinion, it is a paltry device, a very mean art.'

'Undoubtedly,' replied Darcy, to whom this remark was chiefly addressed, 'there is meanness in *all* the arts which ladies sometimes condescend to employ for captivation. Whatever bears affinity to cunning is despicable.'

Miss Bingley was not so entirely satisfied with this reply as to continue the subject.

Elizabeth joined them again only to say that her sister was worse, and that she could not leave her. Bingley urged Mr. Jones's being sent for immediately; while his sisters, convinced that no country advice could be of any service, recommended an express to town for one of the most eminent physicians. This she would not hear of; but she was not so unwilling to comply with their brother's proposal; and it was settled that Mr. Jones should be sent for early in the morning, if Miss Bennet were not decidedly better. Bingley was quite uncomfortable; his sisters declared that they were miserable. They solaced their wretchedness, however, by duets after supper, while he could find no better relief to his feelings than by giving his housekeeper directions that every possible attention might be paid to the sick lady and her sister.

CHAPTER IX

ELIZABETH passed the chief of the night in her
sister's room, and in the morning had the
pleasure of being able to send a tolerable
answer to the inquiries which she very early
received from Mr. Bingley by a housemaid,
and some time afterwards from the two elegant
ladies who waited on his sisters. In spite of
this amendment, however, she requested to have
a note sent to Longbourn, desiring her mother
to visit Jane, and form her own judgment of her
situation. The note was immediately despatched,
and its contents as quickly complied with. Mrs.
Bennet, accompanied by her two youngest girls,
reached Netherfield soon after the family breakfast.

Had she found Jane in any apparent danger,
Mrs. Bennet would have been very miserable;
but being satisfied on seeing her that her illness
was not alarming, she had no wish of her recovering immediately, as her restoration to health
would probably remove her from Netherfield.
She would not listen, therefore, to her daughter's

proposal of being carried home; neither did the apothecary, who arrived about the same time, think it at all advisable. After sitting a little while with Jane, on Miss Bingley's appearance and invitation, the mother and three daughters all attended her into the breakfast-parlour. Bingley met them with hopes that Mrs. Bennet had not found Miss Bennet worse than she expected.

'Indeed I have, sir,' was her answer. 'She is a great deal too ill to be moved. Mr. Jones says we must not think of moving her. We must trespass a little longer on your kindness.'

'Removed!' cried Bingley. 'It must not be thought of. My sister, I am sure, will not hear of her removal.'

'You may depend upon it, madam,' said Miss Bingley, with cold civility, 'that Miss Bennet shall receive every possible attention while she remains with us.'

Mrs. Bennet was profuse in her acknowledgments.

'I am sure,' she added, 'if it was not for such good friends, I do not know what would become of her, for she is very ill indeed, and suffers a vast deal, though with the greatest patience in the world, which is always the way with her, for she has, without exception, the sweetest temper I ever met with. I often tell my other girls they are nothing to *her*. You have a sweet room here, Mr. Bingley, and a charming prospect over that gravel walk. I do not know a place in the country that is equal to Netherfield. You will not think of quitting it in a hurry, I hope, though you have but a short lease.'

'Whatever I do is done in a hurry,' replied he; 'and therefore, if I should resolve to quit Netherfield, I should probably be off in five minutes. At present, however, I consider myself as quite fixed here.'

'That is exactly what I should have supposed of you,' said Elizabeth.

'You begin to comprehend me, do you?' cried he, turning towards her.

'Oh yes—I understand you perfectly.'

'I wish I might take this for a compliment; but to be so easily seen through, I am afraid, is pitiful.'

'That is as it happens. It does not necessarily follow that a deep, intricate character is more or less estimable than such a one as yours.'

'Lizzy,' cried her mother, 'remember where you are, and do not run on in the wild manner that you are suffered to do at home.'

'I did not know before,' continued Bingley immediately, 'that you were a studier of character. It must be an amusing study.'

'Yes, but intricate characters are the *most* amusing. They have at least that advantage.'

'The country,' said Darcy, 'can in general supply but few subjects for such a study. In a country neighbourhood you move in a very confined and unvarying society.'

'But people themselves alter so much, that there is something new to be observed in them for ever.'

'Yes, indeed,' cried Mrs. Bennet, offended by his manner of mentioning a country neighbourhood. 'I assure you there is quite as much of *that* going on in the country as in town.'

Everybody was surprised, and Darcy, after looking at her for a moment, turned silently away. Mrs. Bennet, who fancied she had gained a complete victory over him, continued her triumph.

'I cannot see that London has any great advantage over the country, for my part, except the shops and public places. The country is a vast deal pleasanter, is not it, Mr. Bingley?'

'When I am in the country,' he replied, 'I never wish to leave it; and when I am in town, it is pretty much the same. They have each their advantages, and I can be equally happy in either.'

'Ay—that is because you have the right disposition. But that gentleman,' looking at

Darcy, 'seemed to think the country was nothing at all.'

'Indeed, mama, you are mistaken,' said Elizabeth, blushing for her mother. 'You quite
mistook Mr. Darcy. He only meant that there
was not such a variety of people to be met with
in the country as in town, which you must
acknowledge to be true.'

'Certainly, my dear, nobody said there were;
but as to not meeting with many people in this
neighbourhood, I believe there are few neigh-
bourhoods larger. I know we dine with four-
and-twenty families.'

Nothing but concern for Elizabeth could
enable Bingley to keep his countenance. His
sister was less delicate, and directed her eye
towards Mr. Darcy with a very expressive smile.
Elizabeth, for the sake of saying something that
might turn her mother's thoughts, now asked
her if Charlotte Lucas had been at Longbourn
since *her* coming away.

'Yes, she called yesterday with her father.
What an agreeable man Sir William is, Mr.
Bingley—is not he? so much the man of
fashion! so genteel and so easy!—He has
always something to say to everybody.—*That*
is my idea of good-breeding; and those persons
who fancy themselves very important, and never
open their mouths, quite mistake the matter.'

'Did Charlotte dine with you?'

'No, she would go home. I fancy she was wanted about the mince-pies. For my part, Mr. Bingley, *I* always keep servants that can do their own work; *my* daughters are brought up differently. But everybody is to judge for themselves, and the Lucases are a very good sort of girls, I assure you. It is a pity they are not handsome! Not that *I* think Charlotte so *very* plain—but then she is our particular friend.'

'She seems a very pleasant young woman,' said Bingley.

'Oh! dear, yes;—but you must own she is very plain. Lady Lucas herself has often said so, and envied me Jane's beauty. I do not like to boast of my own child, but to be sure, Jane— one does not often see anybody better looking. It is what everybody says. I do not trust my own partiality. When she was only fifteen, there was a gentleman at my brother Gardiner's in town so much in love with her that my sister- in-law was sure he would make her an offer before we came away. But, however, he did not. Perhaps he thought her too young. How- ever, he wrote some verses on her, and very pretty they were.'

'And so ended his affection,' said Elizabeth impatiently. 'There has been many a one, I fancy, overcome in the same way. I wonder

who first discovered the efficacy of poetry in
driving away love!'

'I have been used to consider poetry as the
food of love,' said Darcy.

'Of a fine, stout, healthy love it may. Everything nourishes what is strong already. But if
it be only a slight, thin sort of inclination, I am
convinced that one good sonnet will starve it
entirely away.'

Darcy only smiled; and the general pause
which ensued made Elizabeth tremble lest her
mother should be exposing herself again. She
longed to speak, but could think of nothing
to say; and after a short silence Mrs. Bennet
began repeating her thanks to Mr. Bingley
for his kindness to Jane, with an apology for
troubling him also with Lizzy. Mr. Bingley
was unaffectedly civil in his answer, and forced
his younger sister to be civil also, and say what
the occasion required. She performed her part
indeed without much graciousness, but Mrs.
Bennet was satisfied, and soon afterwards ordered
her carriage. Upon this signal, the youngest of
her daughters put herself forward. The two
girls had been whispering to each other during
the whole visit, and the result of it was that
the youngest should tax Mr. Bingley with
having promised on his first coming into the
country to give a ball at Netherfield.

Lydia was a stout, well-grown girl of fifteen, with a fine complexion and good - humoured countenance; a favourite with her mother, whose affection had brought her into public at an early age. She had high animal spirits, and a sort of natural self-consequence, which the attentions of the officers, to whom her uncle's good dinners and her own easy manners recommended her, had increased into assurance. She was very equal, therefore, to address Mr. Bingley on the subject of the ball, and abruptly reminded him of his promise; adding, that it would be the most shameful thing in the world if he did not keep it. His answer to this sudden attack was delightful to her mother's ear—

'I am perfectly ready, I assure you, to keep my engagement; and when your sister is recovered, you shall, if you please, name the very day of the ball. But you would not wish to be dancing while she is ill.'

Lydia declared herself satisfied. 'Oh! yes— it would be much better to wait till Jane was well, and by that time most likely Captain Carter would be at Meryton again. And when you have given *your* ball,' she added, 'I shall insist on their giving one also. I shall tell Colonel Forster it will be quite a shame if he does not.'

Mrs. Bennet and her daughters then departed, and Elizabeth returned instantly to Jane, leaving her own and her relations' behaviour to the remarks of the two ladies and Mr. Darcy; the latter of whom, however, could not be prevailed on to join in their censure of *her*, in spite of all Miss Bingley's witticisms on *fine eyes*.

CHAPTER X

THE day passed much as the day before had
done. Mrs. Hurst and Miss Bingley had spent
some hours of the morning with the invalid,
who continued, though slowly, to mend ; and
in the evening Elizabeth joined their party in
the drawing-room. The loo-table, however, did
not appear. Mr. Darcy was writing, and Miss
Bingley, seated near him, was watching the
progress of his letter and repeatedly calling off
his attention by messages to his sister. Mr.
Hurst and Mr. Bingley were at piquet, and
Mrs. Hurst was observing their game.

Elizabeth took up some needlework, and was
sufficiently amused in attending to what passed
between Darcy and his companion. The per-
petual commendations of the lady, either on his
handwriting, or on the evenness of his lines, or
on the length of his letter, with the perfect
unconcern with which her praises were received,
formed a curious dialogue, and was exactly in
unison with her opinion of each.

'How delighted Miss Darcy will be to receive such a letter!'

He made no answer.

'You write uncommonly fast.'

'You are mistaken.   I write rather slowly.'

'How many letters you must have occasion to write in the course of a year! Letters of business, too!   How odious I should think them!'

'It is fortunate, then, that they fall to my lot instead of to yours.'

'Pray tell your sister that I long to see her.'

'I have already told her so once, by your desire.'

'I am afraid you do not like your pen.   Let me mend it for you.   I mend pens remarkably well.'

'Thank you—but I always mend my own.'

'How can you contrive to write so even?'

He was silent.

'Tell your sister I am delighted to hear of her improvement on the harp; and pray let her know that I am quite in raptures with her beautiful little design for a table, and I think it infinitely superior to Miss Grantley's.'

'Will you give me leave to defer your raptures till I write again?   At present I have not room to do them justice.'

'Oh! it is of no consequence.   I shall see her

in January. But do you always write such charming long letters to her, Mr. Darcy?'

'They are generally long; but whether always charming, it is not for me to determine.'

'It is a rule with me that a person who can write a long letter with ease cannot write ill.'

'That will not do for a compliment to Darcy, Caroline,' cried her brother, 'because he does *not* write with ease. He studies too much for words of four syllables. Do not you, Darcy?'

'My style of writing is very different from yours.'

'Oh!' cried Miss Bingley, 'Charles writes in the most careless way imaginable. He leaves out half his words, and blots the rest.'

'My ideas flow so rapidly that I have not time to express them—by which means my letters sometimes convey no ideas at all to my correspondents.'

'Your humility, Mr. Bingley,' said Elizabeth, 'must disarm reproof.'

'Nothing is more deceitful,' said Darcy, 'than the appearance of humility. It is often only carelessness of opinion, and sometimes an indirect boast.'

'And which of the two do you call *my* little recent piece of modesty?'

'The indirect boast; for you are really proud of your defects in writing, because you consider them as proceeding from a rapidity of thought and carelessness of execution, which, if not estimable, you think at least highly interesting. The power of doing anything with quickness is always much prized by the possessor, and often without any attention to the imperfection of the performance. When you told Mrs. Bennet this morning that if you ever resolved on quitting Netherfield you should be gone in five minutes, you meant it to be a sort of panegyric, of compliment to yourself—and yet what is there so very laudable in a precipitance which must leave very necessary business undone, and can be of no real advantage to yourself or any one else ? '

'Nay,' cried Bingley, 'this is too much, to remember at night all the foolish things that were said in the morning. And yet, upon my honour, I believed what I said of myself to be true, and I believe it at this moment. At least, therefore, I did not assume the character of needless precipitance merely to shew off before the ladies.'

'I dare say you believed it; but I am by no means convinced that you would be gone with such celerity. Your conduct would be quite as dependent on chance as that of any man I know ; and if, as you were mounting your horse, a friend were to say, "Bingley, you had better

stay till next week," you would probably do it,
you would probably not go—and at another
word, might stay a month.'

'You have only proved by this,' cried Elizabeth, 'that Mr. Bingley did not do justice to his
own disposition. You have shewn him off now
much more than he did himself.'

'I am exceedingly gratified,' said Bingley, 'by
your converting what my friend says into a
compliment on the sweetness of my temper.
But I am afraid you are giving it a turn which
that gentleman did by no means intend; for he
would certainly think the better of me if, under
such a circumstance, I were to give a flat denial,
and ride off as fast as I could.'

'Would Mr. Darcy then consider the rashness
of your original intention as atoned for by your
obstinacy in adhering to it?'

'Upon my word, I cannot exactly explain the
matter—Darcy must speak for himself.'

'You expect me to account for opinions which
you chuse to call mine, but which I have never
acknowledged. Allowing the case, however, to
stand according to your representation, you must
remember, Miss Bennet, that the friend who is
supposed to desire his return to the house, and
the delay of his plan, has merely desired it,
asked it without offering one argument in favour
of its propriety.'

'To yield readily—easily—to the *persuasion* of a friend is no merit with you.'

'To yield without conviction is no compliment to the understanding of either.'

'You appear to me, Mr. Darcy, to allow nothing for the influence of friendship and affection. A regard for the requester would often make one readily yield to a request without waiting for arguments to reason one into it. I am not particularly speaking of such a case as you have supposed about Mr. Bingley. We may as well wait, perhaps, till the circumstance occurs before we discuss the discretion of his behaviour thereupon. But in general and ordinary cases between friend and friend, where one of them is desired by the other to change a resolution of no very great moment, should you think ill of that person for complying with the desire, without waiting to be argued into it?'

'Will it not be advisable, before we proceed on this subject, to arrange with rather more precision the degree of importance which is to appertain to this request, as well as the degree of intimacy subsisting between the parties?'

'By all means,' cried Bingley; 'let us hear all the particulars, not forgetting their comparative height and size; for that will have more weight in the argument, Miss Bennet, than you may be aware of. I assure you that, if Darcy were not such a great tall fellow, in comparison with myself, I should not pay him half so much deference. I declare I do not know a more awful object than Darcy, on particular occasions, and in particular places; at his own house especially, and of a Sunday evening, when he has nothing to do.'

Mr. Darcy smiled; but Elizabeth thought she could perceive that he was rather offended, and therefore checked her laugh. Miss Bingley warmly resented the indignity he had received, in an expostulation with her brother for talking such nonsense.

'I see your design, Bingley,' said his friend. 'You dislike an argument, and want to silence this.'

'Perhaps I do. Arguments are too much like disputes. If you and Miss Bennet will defer yours till I am out of the room I shall be very thankful; and then you may say whatever you like of me.'

'What you ask,' said Elizabeth, 'is no sacrifice on my side; and Mr. Darcy had much better finish his letter.'

Mr. Darcy took her advice, and did finish his letter.

When that business was over, he applied to Miss Bingley and Elizabeth for the indulgence of some music. Miss Bingley moved with alac-

rity to the pianoforte; and, after a polite request
that Elizabeth would lead the way, which the
other as politely and more earnestly negatived,
she seated herself.

Mrs. Hurst sang with her sister; and while
they were thus employed, Elizabeth could not
help observing, as she turned over some music-
books that lay on the instrument, how frequently
Mr. Darcy's eyes were fixed on her. She hardly
knew how to suppose that she could be an
object of admiration to so great a man; and yet
that he should look at her because he disliked
her was still more strange. She could only
imagine, however, at last, that she drew his
notice because there was a something about her
more wrong and reprehensible, according to his
ideas of right, than in any other person present.
The supposition did not pain her. She liked
him too little to care for his approbation.

After playing some Italian songs, Miss
Bingley varied the charm by a lively Scotch air;
and soon afterwards Mr. Darcy, drawing near
Elizabeth, said to her—

'Do not you feel a great inclination, Miss
Bennet, to seize such an opportunity of dancing
a reel?'

She smiled, but made no answer. He
repeated the question, with some surprise at
her silence.

'Oh!' said she, 'I heard you before, but I could not immediately determine what to say in reply. You wanted me, I know, to say "Yes," that you might have the pleasure of despising my taste; but I always delight in overthrowing those kind of schemes, and cheating a person of their premeditated contempt. I have, therefore, made up my mind to tell you, that I do not want to dance a reel at all—and now despise me if you dare.'

'Indeed I do not dare.'

Elizabeth, having rather expected to affront him, was amazed at his gallantry; but there was a mixture of sweetness and archness in her manner which made it difficult for her to affront anybody, and Darcy had never been so bewitched by any woman as he was by her. He really believed that, were it not for the inferiority of her connexions, he should be in some danger.

Miss Bingley saw, or suspected enough to be jealous; and her great anxiety for the recovery of her dear friend Jane received some assistance from her desire of getting rid of Elizabeth.

She often tried to provoke Darcy into disliking her guest, by talking of their supposed marriage, and planning his happiness in such an alliance.

'I hope,' said she, as they were walking

together in the shrubbery the next day, 'you will give your mother-in-law a few hints, when this desirable event takes place, as to the advantage of holding her tongue; and if you can compass it, do cure the younger girls of running after the officers.—And, if I may mention so delicate a subject, endeavour to check that little something, bordering on conceit and impertinence, which your lady possesses.'

'Have you anything else to propose for my domestic felicity?'

'Oh! yes. Do let the portraits of your uncle and aunt Philips be placed in the gallery at Pemberley. Put them next to your great-uncle the judge. They are in the same profession, you know; only in different lines. As for your Elizabeth's picture, you must not attempt to have it taken, for what painter could do justice to those beautiful eyes?'

'It would not be easy, indeed, to catch their expression, but their colour and shape, and the eyelashes, so remarkably fine, might be copied.'

At that moment they were met from another walk by Mrs. Hurst and Elizabeth herself.

'I did not know that you intended to walk,' said Miss Bingley, in some confusion, lest they had been overheard.

'You used us abominably ill,' answered Mrs.

Hurst, 'running away without telling us that you were coming out.'

Then, taking the disengaged arm of Mr. Darcy, she left Elizabeth to walk by herself. The path just admitted three. Mr. Darcy felt their rudeness, and immediately said—

'This walk is not wide enough for our party. We had better go into the avenue.'

But Elizabeth, who had not the least inclination to remain with them, laughingly answered—

'No, no; stay where you are. You are charmingly grouped, and appear to uncommon advantage. The picturesque would be spoilt by admitting a fourth. Good-bye.'

She then ran gaily off, rejoicing, as she rambled about, in the hope of being at home again in a day or two. Jane was already so much recovered as to intend leaving her room for a couple of hours that evening.

CHAPTER XI

WHEN the ladies removed after dinner, Elizabeth ran up to her sister, and seeing her well guarded from cold, attended her into the drawing-room, where she was welcomed by her two friends with many professions of pleasure; and Elizabeth had never seen them so agreeable as they were during the hour which passed before the gentlemen appeared. Their powers of conversation were considerable. They could describe an entertainment with accuracy, relate an anecdote with humour, and laugh at their acquaintance with spirit.

But when the gentlemen entered, Jane was no longer the first object; Miss Bingley's eyes were instantly turned towards Darcy, and she had something to say to him before he had advanced many steps. He addressed himself directly to Miss Bennet, with a polite congratulation; Mr. Hurst also made her a slight bow, and said he was 'very glad'; but diffuseness and warmth remained for Bingley's salutation.

He was full of joy and attention. The first half-hour was spent in piling up the fire, lest she should suffer from the change of room; and she removed at his desire to the other side of the fireplace, that she might be farther from the door. He then sat down by her, and talked scarcely to any one else. Elizabeth, at work in the opposite corner, saw it all with great delight.

When tea was over, Mr. Hurst reminded his sister-in-law of the card-table—but in vain. She had obtained private intelligence that Mr. Darcy did not wish for cards; and Mr. Hurst soon found even his open petition rejected. She assured him that no one intended to play, and the silence of the whole party on the subject seemed to justify her. Mr. Hurst had therefore nothing to do but to stretch himself on one of the sofas and go to sleep. Darcy took up a book; Miss Bingley did the same; and Mrs. Hurst, principally occupied in playing with her bracelets and rings, joined now and then in her brother's conversation with Miss Bennet.

Miss Bingley's attention was quite as much engaged in watching Mr. Darcy's progress through *his* book, as in reading her own; and she was perpetually either making some inquiry, or looking at his page. She could not win him, however, to any conversation; he merely answered her question, and read on. At length, quite exhausted by the attempt to be amused with her own book, which she had only chosen because it was the second volume of his, she gave a great yawn and said, 'How pleasant it is to spend an evening in this way! I declare after all there is no enjoyment like reading! How much sooner one tires of anything than of a book! When I have a house of my own, I shall be miserable if I have not an excellent library.'

No one made any reply. She then yawned again, threw aside her book, and cast her eyes round the room in quest of some amusement; when, hearing her brother mentioning a ball to Miss Bennet, she turned suddenly towards him and said—

'By the bye, Charles, are you really serious in meditating a dance at Netherfield? I would advise you, before you determine on it, to consult the wishes of the present party; I am much mistaken if there are not some among us to whom a ball would be rather a punishment than a pleasure.'

'If you mean Darcy,' cried her brother, 'he may go to bed, if he chuses, before it begins—but as for the ball, it is quite a settled thing; and as soon as Nicholls has made white soup enough, I shall send round my cards.'

'I should like balls infinitely better,' she replied, 'if they were carried on in a different manner; but there is something insufferably tedious in the usual process of such a meeting. It would surely be much more rational if conversation instead of dancing made the order of the day.'

'Much more rational, my dear Caroline, I dare say, but it would not be near so much like a ball.'

Miss Bingley made no answer, and soon afterwards got up and walked about the room. Her figure was elegant, and she walked well; but Darcy, at whom it was all aimed, was still inflexibly studious. In the desperation of her feelings, she resolved on one effort more, and turning to Elizabeth, said—

'Miss Eliza Bennet, let me persuade you to follow my example, and take a turn about the room. I assure you it is very refreshing after sitting so long in one attitude.'

Elizabeth was surprised, but agreed to it immediately. Miss Bingley succeeded no less in the real object of her civility: Mr. Darcy looked up. He was as much awake to the novelty of attention in that quarter as Elizabeth herself could be, and unconsciously closed his book. He was directly invited to join their party, but he declined it, observing that he could imagine

but two motives for their chusing to walk up
and down the room together, with either of
which motives his joining them would interfere.
What could he mean? she was dying to know
what could be his meaning—and asked Elizabeth
whether she could at all understand him?

'Not at all,' was her answer; 'but depend upon
it, he means to be severe on us, and our surest
way of disappointing him will be to ask nothing
about it.'

Miss Bingley, however, was incapable of
disappointing Mr. Darcy in anything, and per-
severed, therefore, in requiring an explanation
of his two motives.

'I have not the smallest objection to explaining them,' said he, as soon as she allowed him to
speak. 'You either chuse this method of passing
the evening because you are in each other's
confidence, and have secret affairs to discuss,
or because you are conscious that your figures
appear to the greatest advantage in walking;—
if the first, I should be completely in your way,
and if the second, I can admire you much better
as I sit by the fire.'

'Oh! shocking!' cried Miss Bingley. 'I never
heard anything so abominable. How shall we
punish him for such a speech?'

'Nothing so easy, if you have but the inclination,' said Elizabeth. 'We can all plague and

punish one another. Tease him—laugh at him. Intimate as you are, you must know how it is to be done.'

'But upon my honour I do *not*. I do assure you that my intimacy has not yet taught me *that*. Tease calmness of temper and presence of mind! No, no—I feel he may defy us there. And as to laughter, we will not expose ourselves, if you please, by attempting to laugh without a subject. Mr. Darcy may hug himself.'

'Mr. Darcy is not to be laughed at!' cried Elizabeth. 'That is an uncommon advantage, and uncommon I hope it will continue, for it would be a great loss to *me* to have many such acquaintance. I dearly love a laugh.'

'Miss Bingley,' said he, 'has given me credit for more than can be. The wisest and the best of men—nay, the wisest and best of their actions —may be rendered ridiculous by a person whose first object in life is a joke.'

'Certainly,' replied Elizabeth—'there are such people, but I hope I am not one of *them*. I hope I never ridicule what is wise or good. Follies and nonsense, whims and inconsistencies, *do* divert me, I own, and I laugh at them whenever I can. But these, I suppose, are precisely what you are without.'

'Perhaps that is not possible for any one. But it has been the study of my life to avoid

84

those weaknesses which often expose a strong understanding to ridicule.'

'Such as vanity and pride.'

'Yes, vanity is a weakness indeed. But pride —where there is a real superiority of mind, pride will be always under good regulation.'

Elizabeth turned away to hide a smile.

'Your examination of Mr. Darcy is over, I presume,' said Miss Bingley; 'and pray what is the result?'

'I am perfectly convinced by it that Mr. Darcy has no defect. He owns it himself without disguise.'

'No,' said Darcy, 'I have made no such pretension. I have faults enough, but they are not, I hope, of understanding. My temper I dare not vouch for. It is, I believe, too little yielding—certainly too little for the convenience of the world. I cannot forget the follies and vices of others so soon as I ought, nor their offences against myself. My feelings are not puffed about with every attempt to move them. My temper would perhaps be called resentful. My good opinion once lost is lost for ever.'

'*That* is a failing indeed!' cried Elizabeth. 'Implacable resentment *is* a shade in a character. But you have chosen your fault well. I really cannot *laugh* at it. You are safe from me.'

3 F*

'There is, I believe, in every disposition a tendency to some particular evil — a natural defect, which not even the best education can overcome.'

'And *your* defect is a propensity to hate everybody.'

'And yours,' he replied, with a smile, 'is wilfully to misunderstand them.'

'Do let us have a little music,' cried Miss Bingley, tired of a conversation in which she had no share. 'Louisa, you will not mind my waking Mr. Hurst?'

Her sister made not the smallest objection, and the pianoforte was opened; and Darcy, after a few moments' recollection, was not sorry for it. He began to feel the danger of paying Elizabeth too much attention.

CHAPTER XII

In consequence of an agreement between the sisters, Elizabeth wrote the next morning to her mother, to beg that the carriage might be sent for them in the course of the day. But Mrs. Bennet, who had calculated on her daughters remaining at Netherfield till the following Tuesday, which would exactly finish Jane's week, could not bring herself to receive them with pleasure before. Her answer, therefore, was not propitious, at least not to Elizabeth's wishes, for she was impatient to get home. Mrs. Bennet sent them word that they could not possibly have the carriage before Tuesday; and in her postscript it was added that, if Mr. Bingley and his sister pressed them to stay longer, she could spare them very well. Against staying longer, however, Elizabeth was positively resolved—nor did she much expect it would be asked; and fearful, on the contrary, of being considered as intruding themselves needlessly long, she urged Jane to borrow Mr. Bingley's carriage immediately, and at length it was settled that their original design of leaving Netherfield that morning should be mentioned, and the request made.

The communication excited many professions of concern; and enough was said of wishing them to stay at least till the following day to work on Jane; and till the morrow their going was deferred. Miss Bingley was then sorry that she had proposed the delay, for her jealousy and dislike of one sister much exceeded her affection for the other.

The master of the house heard with real sorrow that they were to go so soon, and repeatedly tried to persuade Miss Bennet that it would not be safe for her—that she was not enough recovered; but Jane was firm where she felt herself to be right.

To Mr. Darcy it was welcome intelligence : Elizabeth had been at Netherfield long enough. She attracted him more than he liked—and Miss Bingley was uncivil to *her*, and more teasing than usual to himself. He wisely resolved to be particularly careful that no sign of admiration should *now* escape him, nothing that could elevate her with the hope of influencing his felicity; sensible that if such an idea had been suggested, his behaviour during the last day must have material weight in confirming or crushing it. Steady to his purpose, he scarcely spoke ten words to her through the whole of Saturday, and though they were at one time left by themselves for half an hour, he adhered most conscientiously to his book, and would not even look at her.

On Sunday, after morning service, the separation, so agreeable to almost all, took place. Miss Bingley's civility to Elizabeth increased at last very rapidly, as well as her affection for Jane; and when they parted, after assuring the latter of the pleasure it would always give her to see her either at Longbourn or Netherfield, and embracing her most tenderly, she even shook hands with the former. Elizabeth took leave of the whole party in the liveliest spirits.

They were not welcomed home very cordially by their mother. Mrs. Bennet wondered at their coming, and thought them very wrong to give so much trouble, and was sure Jane would have caught cold again; but their father, though very laconic in his expressions of pleasure, was really glad to see them; he had felt their importance in the family circle. The evening conversation, when they were all assembled, had lost much of its animation, and almost all its sense, by the absence of Jane and Elizabeth.

They found Mary, as usual, deep in the study of thorough bass and human nature; and had some new extracts to admire, and some new observations of threadbare morality to listen to. Catherine and Lydia had information for them of a different sort. Much had been done and much had been said in the regiment since the preceding Wednesday : several of the officers had dined lately with their uncle, a private had been flogged, and it had actually been hinted that Colonel Forster was going to be married.

CHAPTER XIII

'I HOPE, my dear,' said Mr. Bennet to his wife, as they were at breakfast the next morning, 'that you have ordered a good dinner to-day, because I have reason to expect an addition to our family party.'

'Who do you mean, my dear? I know of nobody that is coming, I am sure, unless Charlotte Lucas should happen to call in—and I hope *my* dinners are good enough for her. I do not believe she often sees such at home.'

'The person of whom I speak is a gentleman, and a stranger.'

Mrs. Bennet's eyes sparkled. 'A gentleman and a stranger! It is Mr. Bingley, I am sure. Why, Jane—you never dropt a word of this; you sly thing! Well, I am sure I shall be extremely glad to see Mr. Bingley. But—good Lord! how unlucky! there is not a bit of fish to be got to-day. Lydia, my love, ring the bell —I must speak to Hill this moment.'

'It is *not* Mr. Bingley,' said her husband;

91

'it is a person whom I never saw in the whole course of my life.'

This roused a general astonishment; and he had the pleasure of being eagerly questioned by his wife and five daughters at once.

After amusing himself some time with their curiosity, he thus explained—

'About a month ago I received this letter; and about a fortnight ago I answered it, for I thought it a case of some delicacy, and requiring early attention. It is from my cousin, Mr. Collins, who, when I am dead, may turn you all out of this house as soon as he pleases.'

'Oh! my dear,' cried his wife, 'I cannot bear to hear that mentioned. Pray do not talk of that odious man. I do think it is the hardest thing in the world, that your estate should be entailed away from your own children; and I am sure, if I had been you, I should have tried long ago to do something or other about it.'

Jane and Elizabeth attempted to explain to her the nature of an entail. They had often attempted it before, but it was a subject on which Mrs. Bennet was beyond the reach of reason, and she continued to rail bitterly against the cruelty of settling an estate away from a family of five daughters, in favour of a man whom nobody cared anything about.

'It certainly is a most iniquitous affair,' said

Mr. Bennet, 'and nothing can clear Mr. Collins from the guilt of inheriting Longbourn. But if you will listen to his letter, you may perhaps be a little softened by his manner of expressing himself.'

'No, that I am sure I shall not; and I think it was very impertinent of him to write to you at all, and very hypocritical. I hate such false friends. Why could not he keep on quarrelling with you, as his father did before him?'

'Why, indeed; he does seem to have had some filial scruples on that head, as you will hear.'

'HUNSFORD, NEAR WESTERHAM, KENT,
'15th October.

'DEAR SIR,—The disagreement subsisting between yourself and my late honoured father always gave me much uneasiness, and since I have had the misfortune to lose him, I have frequently wished to heal the breach; but for some time I was kept back by my own doubts, fearing lest it might seem disrespectful to his memory for me to be on good terms with any one with whom it had always pleased him to be at variance.—"There, Mrs. Bennet."—My mind, however, is now made up on the subject, for having received ordination at Easter, I have been so fortunate as to be distinguished by

93

the patronage of the Right Honourable Lady Catherine de Bourgh, widow of Sir Lewis de Bourgh, whose bounty and beneficence has preferred me to the valuable rectory of this parish, where it shall be my earnest endeavour to demean myself with grateful respect towards her Ladyship, and be ever ready to perform those rites and ceremonies which are instituted by the Church of England. As a clergyman, moreover, I feel it my duty to promote and establish the blessing of peace in all families within the reach of my influence; and on these grounds I flatter myself that my present overtures of goodwill are highly commendable, and that the circumstance of my being next in the entail of Longbourn estate will be kindly overlooked on your side, and not lead you to reject the offered olive-branch. I cannot be otherwise than concerned at being the means of injuring your amiable daughters, and beg leave to apologise for it, as well as to assure you of my readiness to make them every possible amends —but of this hereafter. If you should have no objections to receive me into your house, I propose myself the satisfaction of waiting on you and your family, Monday, November 18th, by four o'clock, and shall probably trespass on your hospitality till the Saturday se'nnight following, which I can do without any inconvenience, as

94

Lady Catherine is far from objecting to my occasional absence on a Sunday, provided that some other clergyman is engaged to do the duty of the day.—I remain, dear sir, with respectful compliments to your lady and daughters, your well-wisher and friend,

'WILLIAM COLLINS.'

'At four o'clock, therefore, we may expect this peace-making gentleman,' said Mr. Bennet, as he folded up the letter. 'He seems to be a most conscientious and polite young man, upon my word, and I doubt not will prove a valuable acquaintance, especially if Lady Catherine should be so indulgent as to let him come to us again.'

'There is some sense in what he says about the girls, however, and if he is disposed to make them any amends, I shall not be the person to discourage him.'

'Though it is difficult,' said Jane, 'to guess in what way he can mean to make us the atonement he thinks our due, the wish is certainly to his credit.'

Elizabeth was chiefly struck with his extraordinary deference for Lady Catherine, and his kind intention of christening, marrying, and burying his parishioners whenever it were required.

95

'He must be an oddity, I think,' said she.
'I cannot make him out. There is something
very pompous in his style.—And what can he
mean by apologising for being next in the entail?—We cannot suppose he would help it if
he could.—Can he be a sensible man, sir?'

'No, my dear; I think not. I have great
hopes of finding him quite the reverse. There
is a mixture of servility and self-importance in
his letter, which promises well. I am impatient
to see him.'

'In point of composition,' said Mary, 'his
letter does not seem defective. The idea of
the olive-branch perhaps is not wholly new, yet
I think it is well expressed.'

To Catherine and Lydia, neither the letter
nor its writer were in any degree interesting.
It was next to impossible that their cousin
should come in a scarlet coat, and it was
now some weeks since they had received pleasure from the society of a man in any other
colour. As for their mother, Mr. Collins's
letter had done away much of her ill-will, and
she was preparing to see him with a degree
of composure which astonished her husband
and daughters.

Mr. Collins was punctual to his time, and
was received with great politeness by the whole
family. Mr. Bennet indeed said little; but

the ladies were ready enough to talk, and Mr.
Collins seemed neither in need of encouragement, nor inclined to be silent himself. He
was a tall, heavy-looking young man of five-
and-twenty. His air was grave and stately,
and his manners were very formal. He had
not been long seated before he complimented
Mrs. Bennet on having so fine a family of
daughters; said he had heard much of their
beauty, but that in this instance fame had fallen
short of the truth; and added, that he did not
doubt her seeing them all in due time well disposed of in marriage. This gallantry was not
much to the taste of some of his hearers; but
Mrs. Bennet, who quarrelled with no compliments, answered most readily—

'You are very kind, I am sure; and I wish
with all my heart it may prove so, for else they
will be destitute enough. Things are settled
so oddly.'

'You allude, perhaps, to the entail of this
estate.'

'Ah! sir, I do indeed. It is a grievous affair
to my poor girls, you must confess. Not that
I mean to find fault with *you*, for such things I
know are all chance in this world. There is no
knowing how estates will go when once they
come to be entailed.'

'I am very sensible, madam, of the hardship

to my fair cousins, and could say much on the subject, but that I am cautious of appearing forward and precipitate. But I can assure the young ladies that I come prepared to admire them. At present I will not say more; but, perhaps, when we are better acquainted——'

He was interrupted by a summons to dinner; and the girls smiled on each other. They were not the only objects of Mr. Collins's admiration. The hall, the dining-room, and all its furniture, were examined and praised; and his commendation of everything would have touched Mrs. Bennet's heart, but for the mortifying supposition of his viewing it all as his own future property. The dinner too in its turn was highly admired; and he begged to know to which of his fair cousins the excellency of its cooking was owing. But here he was set right by Mrs. Bennet, who assured him with some asperity that they were very well able to keep a good cook, and that her daughters had nothing to do in the kitchen. He begged pardon for having displeased her. In a softened tone she declared herself not at all offended; but he continued to apologise for about a quarter of an hour.

CHAPTER XIV

DURING dinner Mr. Bennet scarcely spoke at all; but when the servants were withdrawn, he thought it time to have some conversation with his guest, and therefore started a subject in which he expected him to shine, by observing that he seemed very fortunate in his patroness. Lady Catherine de Bourgh's attention to his wishes, and consideration for his comfort, appeared very remarkable. Mr. Bennet could not have chosen better. Mr. Collins was eloquent in her praise. The subject elevated him to more than usual solemnity of manner, and with a most important aspect he protested that ' he had never in his life witnessed such behaviour in a person of rank—such affability and condescension, as he had himself experienced from Lady Catherine. She had been graciously pleased to approve of both the discourses which he had already had the honour of preaching before her. She had also asked him twice to dine at Rosings, and had sent for him only the Saturday before, to make up her pool of quadrille in the evening.

Lady Catherine was reckoned proud by many people he knew, but *he* had never seen anything but affability in her. She had always spoken to him as she would to any other gentleman; she made not the smallest objection to his joining in the society of the neighbourhood, nor to his leaving his parish occasionally for a week or two, to visit his relations. She had even condescended to advise him to marry as soon as he could, provided he chose with discretion; and had once paid him a visit in his humble parsonage, where she had perfectly approved all the alterations he had been making, and had even vouchsafed to suggest some herself—some shelves in the closets upstairs.'

'That is all very proper and civil, I am sure,' said Mrs. Bennet, 'and I dare say she is a very agreeable woman. It is a pity that great ladies in general are not more like her. Does she live near you, sir?'

'The garden in which stands my humble abode is separated only by a lane from Rosings Park, her ladyship's residence.'

'I think you said she was a widow, sir? has she any family?'

'She has one only daughter, the heiress of Rosings, and of very extensive property.'

'Ah!' cried Mrs. Bennet, shaking her head, 'then she is better off than many girls. And what sort of young lady is she? is she handsome?'

'She is a most charming young lady indeed. Lady Catherine herself says that, in point of true beauty, Miss de Bourgh is far superior to the handsomest of her sex, because there is that in her features which marks the young woman of distinguished birth. She is unfortunately of a sickly constitution, which has prevented her making that progress in many accomplishments which she could not otherwise have failed of, as I am informed by the lady who superintended her education, and who still resides with them. But she is perfectly amiable, and often condescends to drive by my humble abode in her little phaeton and ponies.'

'Has she been presented? I do not remember her name among the ladies at court.'

'Her indifferent state of health unhappily prevents her being in town; and by that means, as I told Lady Catherine myself one day, has deprived the British court of its brightest ornament. Her ladyship seemed pleased with the idea; and you may imagine that I am happy on every occasion to offer those little delicate compliments which are always acceptable to ladies. I have more than once observed to Lady Catherine, that her charming daughter seemed born to be a duchess, and that the most elevated rank, instead of giving her consequence, would be adorned by her. These are the kind of little things which please her ladyship, and it is a sort of attention which I conceive myself peculiarly bound to pay.'

'You judge very properly,' said Mr. Bennet, 'and it is happy for you that you possess the talent of flattering with delicacy. May I ask whether these pleasing attentions proceed from the impulse of the moment, or are the result of previous study?'

'They arise chiefly from what is passing at the time, and though I sometimes amuse myself with suggesting and arranging such little elegant compliments as may be adapted to ordinary occasions, I always wish to give them as unstudied an air as possible.'

Mr. Bennet's expectations were fully answered. His cousin was as absurd as he had hoped, and he listened to him with the keenest enjoyment, maintaining at the same time the most resolute composure of countenance, and, except in an occasional glance at Elizabeth, requiring no partner in his pleasure.

By tea-time, however, the dose had been enough, and Mr. Bennet was glad to take his guest into the drawing-room again, and, when tea was over, glad to invite him to read aloud to the ladies. Mr. Collins readily assented, and a book was produced ; but on beholding it (for everything announced it to be from a circulating library) he started back, and begging pardon, protested that he never read novels. Kitty stared at him, and Lydia exclaimed. Other books were produced, and after some deliberation he chose Fordyce's Sermons. Lydia gaped as he opened the volume, and before he had, with very monotonous solemnity, read three pages, she interrupted him with—

'Do you know, mama, that my uncle Philips talks of turning away Richard ; and if he does, Colonel Forster will hire him. My aunt told me so herself on Saturday. I shall walk to Meryton to-morrow to hear more about it, and to ask when Mr. Denny comes back from town.'

Lydia was bid by her two eldest sisters to hold her tongue ; but Mr. Collins, much offended, laid aside his book, and said—

'I have often observed how little young ladies are interested by books of a serious stamp, though written solely for their benefit. It amazes me, I confess ; for, certainly, there can be nothing so advantageous to them as instruction. But I will no longer importune my young cousin.'

Then, turning to Mr. Bennet, he offered himself as his antagonist at backgammon. Mr. Bennet accepted the challenge, observing that he acted very wisely in leaving the girls to their own trifling amusements. Mrs. Bennet and her daughters apologised most civilly for Lydia's interruption, and promised that it should not occur again, if he would resume his book; but Mr. Collins, after assuring them that he bore his young cousin no ill-will, and should never resent her behaviour as any affront, seated himself at another table with Mr. Bennet, and prepared for backgammon.

CHAPTER XV

MR. COLLINS was not a sensible man, and the deficiency of nature had been but little assisted by education or society; the greatest part of his life having been spent under the guidance of an illiterate and miserly father; and though he belonged to one of the universities, he had merely kept the necessary terms, without forming at it any useful acquaintance. The subjection in which his father had brought him up had given him originally great humility of manner; but it was now a good deal counteracted by the self-conceit of a weak head, living in retirement, and the consequential feelings of early and unexpected prosperity. A fortunate chance had recommended him to Lady Catherine de Bourgh when the living of Hunsford was vacant; and the respect which he felt for her high rank, and his veneration for her as his patroness, mingling with a very good opinion of himself, of his authority as a clergyman, and his right as a rector, made him altogether a mixture of pride and obsequiousness, self-importance, and humility.

Having now a good house and very sufficient income, he intended to marry; and in seeking a reconciliation with the Longbourn family he had a wife in view, as he meant to chuse one of the daughters, if he found them as handsome and amiable as they were represented by common report. This was his plan of amends—of atonement—for inheriting their father's estate; and he thought it an excellent one, full of eligibility and suitableness, and excessively generous and disinterested on his own part.

His plan did not vary on seeing them. Miss Bennet's lovely face confirmed his views, and established all his strictest notions of what was due to seniority; and for the first evening *she* was his settled choice. The next morning, however, made an alteration; for in a quarter-of-an-hour's *tête-à-tête* with Mrs. Bennet before breakfast, a conversation beginning with his parsonage-house, and leading naturally to the avowal of his hopes, that a mistress for it might be found at Longbourn, produced from her, amid very complaisant smiles and general encouragement, a caution against the very Jane he had fixed on. 'As to her *younger* daughters, she could not take upon her to say—she could not positively answer—but she did not *know* of any prepossession; her *eldest* daughter, she must just mention—she felt it incumbent on her to hint, was likely to be very soon engaged.'

Mr. Collins had only to change from Jane to Elizabeth—and it was soon done—done while Mrs. Bennet was stirring the fire. Elizabeth, equally next to Jane in birth and beauty, succeeded her of course.

Mrs. Bennet treasured up the hint, and trusted that she might soon have two daughters married; and the man whom she could not bear to speak of the day before was now high in her good graces.

Lydia's intention of walking to Meryton was not forgotten; every sister except Mary agreed to go with her; and Mr. Collins was to attend them, at the request of Mr. Bennet, who was most anxious to get rid of him, and have his library to himself; for thither Mr. Collins had followed him after breakfast, and there he would continue, nominally engaged with one of the largest folios in the collection, but really talking to Mr. Bennet, with little cessation, of his house and garden at Hunsford. Such doings discomposed Mr. Bennet exceedingly. In his library he had been always sure of leisure and tranquillity; and though prepared, as he told Elizabeth, to meet with folly and conceit in every other room in the house, he was used to be free from them there; his civility, therefore, was most prompt in inviting Mr. Collins to join his daughters in their walk; and Mr. Collins, being in fact much better fitted for a walker than a reader, was extremely well pleased to close his large book, and go.

In pompous nothings on his side, and civil assents on that of his cousins, their time passed till they entered Meryton. The attention of the younger ones was then no longer to be gained by *him*. Their eyes were immediately wandering up in the street in quest of the officers, and nothing less than a very smart bonnet indeed, or a really new muslin in a shop window, could recall them.

But the attention of every lady was soon caught by a young man, whom they had never seen before, of most gentlemanlike appearance, walking with an officer on the other side of the way. The officer was the very Mr. Denny concerning whose return from London Lydia came to inquire, and he bowed as they passed. All were struck with the stranger's air, all wondered who he could be; and Kitty and Lydia, determined if possible to find out, led the way across the street, under pretence of wanting something in an opposite shop, and fortunately had just gained the pavement when the two gentlemen, turning back, had reached the same spot. Mr.

Denny addressed them directly, and entreated permission to introduce his friend, Mr. Wickham, who had returned with him the day before from town, and he was happy to say had accepted a commission in their corps. This was exactly as it should be; for the young man wanted only regimentals to make him completely charming. His appearance was greatly in his favour; he had all the best part of beauty, a fine countenance, a good figure, and very pleasing address. The introduction was followed up on his side by a happy readiness of conversation—a readiness at the same time perfectly correct and unassuming; and the whole party were still standing and talking together very agreeably, when the sound of horses drew their notice, and Darcy and Bingley were seen riding down the street. On distinguishing the ladies of the group the two gentlemen came directly towards them, and began the usual civilities. Bingley was the principal spokesman, and Miss Bennet the principal object. He was then, he said, on his way to Longbourn on purpose to inquire after her. Mr. Darcy corroborated it with a bow, and was beginning to determine not to fix his eyes on Elizabeth, when they were suddenly arrested by the sight of the stranger, and Elizabeth, happening to see the countenance of both as they looked at each other, was all astonishment at the effect of the meeting. Both changed colour; one looked white, the other red. Mr. Wickham, after a few moments, touched his hat—a salutation which Mr. Darcy just deigned to return. What could be the meaning of it?—It was impossible to imagine; it was impossible not to long to know.

In another minute Mr. Bingley, but without seeming to have noticed what passed, took leave and rode on with his friend.

Mr. Denny and Mr. Wickham walked with the young ladies to the door of Mr. Philips's house, and then made their bows, in spite of Miss Lydia's pressing entreaties that they would come in, and even in spite of Mrs. Philips's throwing up the parlour window and loudly seconding the invitation.

Mrs. Philips was always glad to see her nieces; and the two eldest, from their recent absence, were particularly welcome, and she was eagerly expressing her surprise at their sudden return home, which, as their own carriage had not fetched them, she should have known nothing about, if she had not happened to see Mr. Jones's shop-boy in the street, who had told her that they were not to send any more draughts to Netherfield because the Miss Bennets were come away, when her civility was claimed towards Mr. Collins by Jane's introduction of

him. She received him with her very best
politeness, which he returned with as much
more, apologising for his intrusion, without any
previous acquaintance with her, which he could
not help flattering himself, however, might be
justified by his relationship to the young ladies
who introduced him to her notice. Mrs. Philips
was quite awed by such an excess of good-
breeding; but her contemplation of one stranger
was soon put an end to by exclamations and
inquiries about the other; of whom, however,
she could only tell her nieces what they already
knew, that Mr. Denny had brought him from
London, and that he was to have a lieutenant's
commission in the ——shire. She had been
watching him the last hour, she said, as he
walked up and down the street, and had Mr.
Wickham appeared, Kitty and Lydia would
certainly have continued the occupation, but
unluckily no one passed the windows now except
a few of the officers, who, in comparison with
the stranger, were become 'stupid, disagreeable
fellows.' Some of them were to dine with the
Philipses the next day, and their aunt promised
to make her husband call on Mr. Wickham,
and give him an invitation also, if the family
from Longbourn would come in the evening.
This was agreed to, and Mrs. Philips protested
that they would have a nice comfortable noisy

game of lottery tickets, and a little bit of hot supper afterwards. The prospect of such delights was very cheering, and they parted in mutual good spirits. Mr. Collins repeated his apologies in quitting the room, and was assured with unwearying civility that they were perfectly needless.

As they walked home, Elizabeth related to Jane what she had seen pass between the two gentlemen; but though Jane would have defended either or both, had they appeared to be wrong, she could no more explain such behaviour than her sister.

Mr. Collins on his return highly gratified Mrs. Bennet by admiring Mrs. Philips's manners and politeness. He protested that, except Lady Catherine and her daughter, he had never seen a more elegant woman; for she had not only received him with the utmost civility, but had even pointedly included him in her invitation for the next evening, although utterly unknown to her before. Something, he supposed, might be attributed to his connexion with them, but yet he had never met with so much attention in the whole course of his life.

CHAPTER XVI

As no objection was made to the young people's engagement with their aunt, and all Mr. Collins's scruples of leaving Mr. and Mrs. Bennet for a single evening during his visit were most steadily resisted, the coach conveyed him and his five cousins at a suitable hour to Meryton; and the girls had the pleasure of hearing, as they entered the drawing-room, that Mr. Wickham had accepted their uncle's invitation, and was then in the house.

When this information was given, and they had all taken their seats, Mr. Collins was at leisure to look around him and admire, and he was so much struck with the size and furniture of the apartment, that he declared he might almost have supposed himself in the small summer breakfast-parlour at Rosings; a comparison that did not at first convey much gratification; but when Mrs. Philips understood from him what Rosings was, and who was its proprietor—when she had listened to the description of only one of Lady Catherine's drawing-

rooms, and found that the chimney-piece alone
had cost eight hundred pounds, she felt all the
force of the compliment, and would hardly have
resented a comparison with the housekeeper's
room.

In describing to her all the grandeur of Lady
Catherine and her mansion, with occasional
digressions in praise of his own humble abode,
and the improvements it was receiving, he was
happily employed until the gentlemen joined
them; and he found in Mrs. Philips a very
attentive listener, whose opinion of his consequence increased with what she heard, and
who was resolving to retail it all among her
neighbours as soon as she could. To the girls,
who could not listen to their cousin, and who
had nothing to do but to wish for an instrument,
and examine their own indifferent imitations of
china on the mantelpiece, the interval of waiting
appeared very long. It was over at last, however. The gentlemen did approach, and when
Mr. Wickham walked into the room, Elizabeth
felt that she had neither been seeing him before,
nor thinking of him since, with the smallest
degree of unreasonable admiration. The officers
of the ——shire were in general a very credit-
able, gentlemanlike set, and the best of them
were of the present party; but Mr. Wickham
was as far beyond them all in person, counten-

ance, air, and walk, as *they* were superior to the
broad-faced, stuffy uncle Philips, breathing port
wine, who followed them into the room.

Mr. Wickham was the happy man towards
whom almost every female eye was turned, and
Elizabeth was the happy woman by whom he
finally seated himself; and the agreeable manner
in which he immediately fell into conversation,
though it was only on its being a wet night, and
on the probability of a rainy season, made her
feel that the commonest, dullest, most threadbare topic might be rendered interesting by the
skill of the speaker.

With such rivals for the notice of the fair
as Mr. Wickham and the officers, Mr. Collins
seemed to sink into insignificance; to the young
ladies he certainly was nothing; but he had
still at intervals a kind listener in Mrs. Philips,
and was, by her watchfulness, most abundantly
supplied with coffee and muffin.

When the card-tables were placed, he had an
opportunity of obliging her in return, by sitting
down to whist.

' I know little of the game at present,' said he,
' but I shall be glad to improve myself, for in
my situation in life——' Mrs. Philips was very
thankful for his compliance, but could not wait
for his reason.

Mr. Wickham did not play at whist, and with

ready delight was he received at the other table
between Elizabeth and Lydia. At first there
seemed danger of Lydia's engrossing him entirely,
for she was a most determined talker; but being
likewise extremely fond of lottery tickets, she
soon grew too much interested in the game, too
eager in making bets and exclaiming after prizes,
to have attention for any one in particular.
Allowing for the common demands of the game,
Mr. Wickham was therefore at leisure to talk
to Elizabeth, and she was very willing to hear
him, though what she chiefly wished to hear
she could not hope to be told—the history of his
acquaintance with Mr. Darcy. She dared not
even mention that gentleman. Her curiosity,
however, was unexpectedly relieved. Mr.
Wickham began the subject himself. He inquired how far Netherfield was from Meryton;
and after receiving her answer, asked in a hesi-
tating manner how long Mr. Darcy had been
staying there.

'About a month,' said Elizabeth; and then,
unwilling to let the subject drop, added, 'He
is a man of very large property in Derbyshire,
I understand.'

'Yes,' replied Wickham; 'his estate there is
a noble one. A clear ten thousand per annum.
You could not have met with a person more
capable of giving you certain information on

that head than myself; for I have been connected with his family in a particular manner from my infancy.'

Elizabeth could not but look surprised.

'You may well be surprised, Miss Bennet, at such an assertion, after seeing, as you probably might, the very cold manner of our meeting yesterday. Are you much acquainted with Mr. Darcy?'

'As much as I ever wish to be,' cried Elizabeth warmly. 'I have spent four days in the same house with him, and I think him very disagreeable.'

'I have no right to give *my* opinion,' said Wickham, 'as to his being agreeable or otherwise. I am not qualified to form one. I have known him too long and too well to be a fair judge. It is impossible for *me* to be impartial. But I believe your opinion of him would in general astonish—and perhaps you would not express it quite so strongly anywhere else. Here you are in your own family.'

'Upon my word, I say no more *here* than I might say in any house in the neighbourhood, except Netherfield. He is not at all liked in Hertfordshire. Everybody is disgusted with his pride. You will not find him more favourably spoken of by any one.'

'I cannot pretend to be sorry,' said Wickham,

after a short interruption, 'that he or that any man should not be estimated beyond their deserts; but with *him* I believe it does not often happen. The world is blinded by his fortune and consequence, or frightened by his high and imposing manners, and sees him only as he chuses to be seen.'

'I should take him, even on *my* slight acquaintance, to be an ill-tempered man.' Wickham only shook his head.

'I wonder,' said he, at the next opportunity of speaking, 'whether he is likely to be in this country much longer.'

'I do not at all know; but I *heard* nothing of his going away when I was at Netherfield. I hope your plans in favour of the ——shire will not be affected by his being in the neighbourhood.'

'Oh! no—it is not for *me* to be driven away by Mr. Darcy. If *he* wishes to avoid seeing *me*, he must go. We are not on friendly terms, and it always gives me pain to meet him, but I have no reason for avoiding *him* but what I might proclaim before all the world—a sense of very great ill-usage, and most painful regrets at his being what he is. His father, Miss Bennet, the late Mr. Darcy, was one of the best men that ever breathed, and the truest friend I ever had; and I can never be in company with this Mr.

Darcy without being grieved to the soul by a thousand tender recollections. His behaviour to myself has been scandalous; but I verily believe I could forgive him anything and everything, rather than his disappointing the hopes and disgracing the memory of his father.'

Elizabeth found the interest of the subject increase, and listened with all her heart; but the delicacy of it prevented farther inquiry.

Mr. Wickham began to speak on more general topics, Meryton, the neighbourhood, the society, appearing highly pleased with all that he had yet seen, and speaking of the latter especially with gentle but very intelligible gallantry.

'It was the prospect of constant society, and good society,' he added, 'which was my chief inducement to enter the ——shire. I knew it to be a most respectable, agreeable corps, and my friend Denny tempted me farther by his account of their present quarters, and the very great attentions and excellent acquaintance Meryton had procured them. Society, I own, is necessary to me. I have been a disappointed man, and my spirits will not bear solitude. I *must* have employment and society. A military life is not what I was intended for, but circumstances have now made it eligible. The church *ought* to have been my profession—I was brought up for the church, and I should at this time have been in possession of a most valuable living, had it pleased the gentleman we were speaking of just now.'

'Indeed!'

'Yes—the late Mr. Darcy bequeathed me the next presentation of the best living in his gift. He was my godfather, and excessively attached to me. I cannot do justice to his kindness. He meant to provide for me amply, and thought he had done it; but when the living fell it was given elsewhere.'

'Good heavens!' cried Elizabeth; 'but how could *that* be?—How could his will be disregarded?—Why did not you seek legal redress?'

'There was just such an informality in the terms of the bequest as to give me no hope from law. A man of honour could not have doubted the intention, but Mr. Darcy chose to doubt it —or to treat it as a merely conditional recommendation, and to assert that I had forfeited all claim to it by extravagance, imprudence—in short, anything or nothing. Certain it is, that the living became vacant two years ago, exactly as I was of an age to hold it, and that it was given to another man; and no less certain is it, that I cannot accuse myself of having really done anything to deserve to lose it. I have a warm, unguarded temper, and I may perhaps

120

have sometimes spoken my opinion *of* him, and *to* him, too freely. I can recall nothing worse. But the fact is, that we are very different sort of men, and that he hates me.'

'This is quite shocking!—He deserves to be publicly disgraced.'

'Some time or other he *will* be—but it shall not be by *me*. Till I can forget his father I can never defy or expose *him*.'

Elizabeth honoured him for such feelings, and thought him handsomer than ever as he expressed them.

'But what,' said she, after a pause, 'can have been his motive?—what can have induced him to behave so cruelly?'

'A thorough, determined dislike of me—a dislike which I cannot but attribute in some measure to jealousy. Had the late Mr. Darcy liked me less, his son might have borne with me better; but his father's uncommon attachment to me irritated him, I believe, very early in life. He had not a temper to bear the sort of competition in which we stood—the sort of preference which was often given me.'

'I had not thought Mr. Darcy so bad as this —though I have never liked him, I had not thought so very ill of him.—I had supposed him to be despising his fellow-creatures in general, but did not suspect him of descending to such

121

malicious revenge, such injustice, such inhumanity as this.'

After a few minutes' reflection, however, she continued—'I *do* remember his boasting one day, at Netherfield, of the implacability of his resentments, of his having an unforgiving temper. His disposition must be dreadful.'

'I will not trust myself on the subject,' replied Wickham; '*I* can hardly be just to him.'

Elizabeth was again deep in thought, and after a time exclaimed, 'To treat in such a manner the godson, the friend, the favourite of his father!'—She could have added, 'A young man, too, like *you*, whose very countenance may vouch for your being amiable'—but she contented herself with, 'And one, too, who had probably been his own companion from childhood, connected together, as I think you said, in the closest manner!'

'We were born in the same parish, within the same park; the greatest part of our youth was passed together; inmates of the same house, sharing the same amusements, objects of the same parental care. *My* father began life in the profession which your uncle, Mr. Philips, appears to do so much credit to—but he gave up everything to be of use to the late Mr. Darcy, and devoted all his time to the care of the Pemberley property. He was most highly esteemed by

122

Mr. Darcy, a most intimate, confidential friend. Mr. Darcy often acknowledged himself to be under the greatest obligations to my father's active superintendence, and when, immediately before my father's death, Mr. Darcy gave him a voluntary promise of providing for me, I am convinced that he felt it to be as much a debt of gratitude to *him* as of affection to myself.'

'How strange!' cried Elizabeth. 'How abominable!—I wonder that the very pride of this Mr. Darcy has not made him just to you!— If from no better motive, that he should not have been too proud to be dishonest—for dishonesty I must call it.'

'It *is* wonderful,' replied Wickham,—'for almost all his actions may be traced to pride; and pride has often been his best friend. It has connected him nearer with virtue than any other feeling. But we are none of us consistent, and in his behaviour to me there were stronger impulses even than pride.'

'Can such abominable pride as his have ever done him good?'

'Yes. It has often led him to be liberal and generous—to give his money freely, to display hospitality, to assist his tenants, and relieve the poor. Family pride, and *filial* pride—for he is very proud of what his father was—have done this. Not to appear to disgrace his family, to degenerate from the popular qualities, or lose the influence of the Pemberley House, is a powerful motive. He has also *brotherly* pride, which, with *some* brotherly affection, makes him a very kind and careful guardian of his sister, and you will hear him generally cried up as the most attentive and best of brothers.'

'What sort of a girl is Miss Darcy?'

He shook his head. 'I wish I could call her amiable. It gives me pain to speak ill of a Darcy. But she is too much like her brother—very, very proud. As a child, she was affectionate and pleasing, and extremely fond of me; and I have devoted hours and hours to her amusement. But she is nothing to me now. She is an handsome girl, about fifteen or sixteen, and I understand, highly accomplished. Since her father's death, her home has been London, where a lady lives with her, and superintends her education.'

After many pauses and many trials of other subjects, Elizabeth could not help reverting once more to the first, and saying—

'I am astonished at his intimacy with Mr. Bingley! How can Mr. Bingley, who seems good-humour itself, and is, I really believe, truly amiable, be in friendship with such a man? How can they suit each other? Do you know Mr. Bingley?'

‘ Not at all.’

‘He is a sweet-tempered, amiable, charming man. He cannot know what Mr. Darcy is.’

‘Probably not;—but Mr. Darcy can please where he chuses. He does not want abilities. He can be a conversible companion if he thinks it worth his while. Among those who are at all his equals in consequence, he is a very different man from what he is to the less prosperous. His pride never deserts him : but with the rich he is liberal-minded, just, sincere, rational, honourable, and perhaps agreeable — allowing something for fortune and figure.’

The whist party soon afterwards breaking up, the players gathered round the other table, and Mr. Collins took his station between his cousin Elizabeth and Mrs. Philips. The usual inquiries as to his success were made by the latter. It had not been very great : he had lost every point; but when Mrs. Philips began to express her concern thereupon, he assured her with much earnest gravity that it was not of the least importance, that he considered the money as a mere trifle, and begged she would not make herself uneasy.

‘I know very well, madam,’ said he, ‘that when persons sit down to a card-table they must take their chance of these things—and happily I am not in such circumstances as to make five shillings any object. There are undoubtedly many who could not say the same, but thanks to Lady Catherine de Bourgh, I am removed far beyond the necessity of regarding little matters.'

Mr. Wickham's attention was caught; and after observing Mr. Collins for a few moments, he asked Elizabeth in a low voice whether her relation were very intimately acquainted with the family of De Bourgh.

'Lady Catherine de Bourgh,' she replied, 'has very lately given him a living. I hardly know how Mr. Collins was first introduced to her notice, but he certainly has not known her long.'

'You know of course that Lady Catherine de Bourgh and Lady Anne Darcy were sisters; consequently that she is aunt to the present Mr. Darcy.'

'No, indeed, I did not. I knew nothing at all of Lady Catherine's connexions. I never heard of her existence till the day before yesterday.'

'Her daughter, Miss de Bourgh, will have a very large fortune, and it is believed that she and her cousin will unite the two estates.'

This information made Elizabeth smile, as she thought of poor Miss Bingley. Vain indeed must be all her attentions, vain and useless her affection for his sister and her praise of himself, if he were already self-destined to another.

'Mr. Collins,' said she, 'speaks highly both of Lady Catherine and her daughter; but from some particulars that he has related of her lady-ship, I suspect his gratitude misleads him, and that in spite of her being his patroness, she is an arrogant, conceited woman.'

'I believe her to be both in a great degree,' replied Wickham; 'I have not seen her for many years, but I very well remember that I never liked her, and that her manners were dictatorial and insolent. She has the reputation of being remarkably sensible and clever; but I rather believe she derives part of her abilities from her rank and fortune, part from her authori-tative manner, and the rest from the pride of her nephew, who chuses that every one con-nected with him should have an understanding of the first class.'

Elizabeth allowed that he had given a very rational account of it, and they continued talk-ing together with mutual satisfaction till supper put an end to cards, and gave the rest of the ladies their share of Mr. Wickham's attentions. There could be no conversation in the noise of Mrs. Philips's supper party, but his manners recommended him to everybody. Whatever he said, was said well; and whatever he did, done gracefully. Elizabeth went away with her head full of him. She could think of nothing but of Mr. Wickham, and of what he had told her, all the way home ; but there was not time for her even to mention his name as they went, for neither Lydia nor Mr. Collins were once silent. Lydia talked incessantly of lottery tickets, of the fish she had lost and the fish she had won ; and Mr. Collins, in describing the civility of Mr. and Mrs. Philips, protesting that he did not in the least regard his losses at whist, enumerating all the dishes at supper, and repeatedly fearing that he crowded his cousins, had more to say than he could well manage before the carriage stopped at Longbourn House.

CHAPTER XVII

ELIZABETH related to Jane the next day what had passed between Mr. Wickham and herself. Jane listened with astonishment and concern; she knew not how to believe that Mr. Darcy could be so unworthy of Mr. Bingley's regard; and yet, it was not in her nature to question the veracity of a young man of such amiable appearance as Wickham. The possibility of his having really endured such unkindness, was enough to interest all her tender feelings; and nothing therefore remained to be done, but to think well of them both, to defend the conduct of each, and throw into the account of accident or mistake whatever could not be otherwise explained.

'They have both,' said she, 'been deceived, I dare say, in some way or other, of which we can form no idea. Interested people have perhaps misrepresented each to the other. It is, in short, impossible for us to conjecture the causes or circumstances which may have alienated them, without actual blame on either side.'

'Very true, indeed;—and now, my dear Jane, what have you got to say in behalf of the interested people who have probably been concerned in the business? Do clear *them* too, or we shall be obliged to think ill of somebody.'

'Laugh as much as you chuse, but you will not laugh me out of my opinion. My dearest Lizzy, do but consider in what a disgraceful light it places Mr. Darcy, to be treating his father's favourite in such a manner—one whom his father had promised to provide for. It is impossible. No man of common humanity, no man who had any value for his character, could be capable of it. Can his most intimate friends be so excessively deceived in him?—oh! no.'

'I can much more easily believe Mr. Bingley's being imposed on, than that Mr. Wickham should invent such an history of himself as he gave me last night; names, facts, everything mentioned without ceremony. If it be not so, let Mr. Darcy contradict it. Besides, there was truth in his looks.'

'It is difficult indeed—it is distressing. One does not know what to think.'

'I beg your pardon; one knows exactly what to think.'

But Jane could think with certainty on only one point—that Mr. Bingley, if he *had been* imposed on, would have much to suffer when the affair became public.

The two young ladies were summoned from the shrubbery, where this conversation passed, by the arrival of some of the very persons of whom they had been speaking: Mr. Bingley and his sisters came to give their personal invitation for the long-expected ball at Netherfield, which was fixed for the following Tuesday. The two ladies were delighted to see their dear friend again—called it an age since they had met, and repeatedly asked what she had been doing with herself since their separation. To the rest of the family they paid little attention: avoiding Mrs. Bennet as much as possible, saying not much to Elizabeth, and nothing at all to the others. They were soon gone again, rising from their seats with an activity which took their brother by surprise, and hurrying off as if eager to escape from Mrs. Bennet's civilities.

The prospect of the Netherfield ball was extremely agreeable to every female of the family. Mrs. Bennet chose to consider it as given in compliment to her eldest daughter, and was particularly flattered by receiving the invitation from Mr. Bingley himself, instead of a ceremonious card. Jane pictured to herself a happy evening in the society of her two friends, and the attentions of their brother ; and Elizabeth thought with pleasure of dancing a great deal with Mr. Wickham, and of seeing a confirmation of everything in Mr. Darcy's look and behaviour. The happiness anticipated by Catherine and Lydia depended less on any single event, or any particular person; for though they each, like Elizabeth, meant to dance half the evening with Mr. Wickham, he was by no means the only partner who could satisfy them, and a ball was, at any rate, a ball. And even Mary could assure her family that she had no disinclination for it.

'While I can have my mornings to myself,' said she, 'it is enough—I think it is no sacrifice to join occasionally in evening engagements. Society has claims on us all; and I profess myself one of those who consider intervals of recreation and amusement as desirable for everybody.'

Elizabeth's spirits were so high on the occasion that, though she did not often speak unnecessarily to Mr. Collins, she could not help asking him whether he intended to accept Mr. Bingley's invitation, and if he did, whether he would think it proper to join in the evening's amusement; and she was rather surprised to find that he entertained no scruple whatever on that head, and was very far from dreading a rebuke either from the Archbishop or

Lady Catherine de Bourgh, by venturing to dance.

'I am by no means of opinion, I assure you,' said he, 'that a ball of this kind, given by a young man of character, to respectable people, can have any evil tendency; and I am so far from objecting to dancing myself, that I shall hope to be honoured with the hands of all my fair cousins in the course of the evening; and I take this opportunity of soliciting yours, Miss Elizabeth, for the two first dances especially— a preference which I trust my cousin Jane will attribute to the right cause, and not to any disrespect for her.'

Elizabeth felt herself completely taken in. She had fully proposed being engaged by Mr. Wickham for those very dances; and to have Mr. Collins instead!—her liveliness had been never worse timed. There was no help for it, however. Mr. Wickham's happiness and her own was per force delayed a little longer, and Mr. Collins's proposal accepted with as good a grace as she could. She was not the better pleased with his gallantry from the idea it suggested of something more. It now first struck her that *she* was selected from among her sisters as worthy of being the mistress of Hunsford Parsonage, and of assisting to form a quadrille table at Rosings, in the absence of more eligible visitors. The idea soon reached to conviction, as she observed his increasing civilities towards herself, and heard his frequent attempt at a compliment on her wit and vivacity; and though more astonished than gratified herself by this effect of her charms, it was not long before her mother gave her to understand that the probability of their marriage was exceedingly agreeable to *her*. Elizabeth, however, did not chuse to take the hint, being well aware that a serious dispute must be the consequence of any reply. Mr. Collins might never make the offer, and, till he did, it was useless to quarrel about him.

If there had not been a Netherfield ball to prepare for and talk of, the younger Miss Bennets would have been in a pitiable state at this time; for, from the day of the invitation to the day of the ball, there was such a succession of rain as prevented their walking to Meryton once. No aunt, no officers, no news could be sought after—the very shoe-roses for Netherfield were got by proxy. Even Elizabeth might have found some trial of her patience in weather which totally suspended the improvement of her acquaintance with Mr. Wickham; and nothing less than a dance on Tuesday could have made such a Friday, Saturday, Sunday, and Monday endurable to Kitty and Lydia.

CHAPTER XVIII

TILL Elizabeth entered the drawing-room at Netherfield, and looked in vain for Mr. Wickham among the cluster of red coats there assembled, a doubt of his being present had never occurred to her. The certainty of meeting him had not been checked by any of those recollections that might not unreasonably have alarmed her. She had dressed with more than usual care, and prepared in the highest spirits for the conquest of all that remained unsubdued of his heart, trusting that it was not more than might be won in the course of the evening. But in an instant arose the dreadful suspicion of his being purposely omitted for Mr. Darcy's pleasure in the Bingleys' invitation to the officers; and though this was not exactly the case, the absolute fact of his absence was pronounced by his friend Mr. Denny, to whom Lydia eagerly applied, and who told them that Wickham had been obliged to go to town on business the day before, and was not yet returned; adding, with a significant smile—

'I do not imagine his business would have called him away just now, if he had not wished to avoid a certain gentleman here.'

This part of his intelligence, though unheard by Lydia, was caught by Elizabeth, and as it assured her that Darcy was not less answerable for Wickham's absence than if her first surmise had been just, every feeling of displeasure against the former was so sharpened by immediate disappointment, that she could hardly reply with tolerable civility to the polite inquiries which he directly afterwards approached to make. Attention, forbearance, patience with Darcy, was injury to Wickham. She was resolved against any sort of conversation with him, and turned away with a degree of ill-humour which she could not wholly surmount even in speaking to Mr. Bingley, whose blind partiality provoked her.

But Elizabeth was not formed for ill-humour; and though every prospect of her own was destroyed for the evening, it could not dwell long on her spirits; and having told all her griefs to Charlotte Lucas, whom she had not seen for a week, she was soon able to make a voluntary transition to the oddities of her cousin, and to point him out to her particular notice. The two first dances, however, brought a return of distress; they were dances of mortification.

Mr. Collins, awkward and solemn, apologising instead of attending, and often moving wrong without being aware of it, gave her all the shame and misery which a disagreeable partner for a couple of dances can give. The moment of her release from him was ecstasy.

She danced next with an officer, and had the refreshment of talking of Wickham, and of hearing that he was universally liked. When those dances were over she returned to Charlotte Lucas, and was in conversation with her when she found herself suddenly addressed by Mr. Darcy, who took her so much by surprise in his application for her hand, that, without knowing what she did, she accepted him. He walked away again immediately, and she was left to fret over her own want of presence of mind ; Charlotte tried to console her.

'I dare say you will find him very agreeable.'

'Heaven forbid! *That* would be the greatest misfortune of all!—To find a man agreeable whom one is determined to hate! Do not wish me such an evil.'

When the dancing recommenced, however, and Darcy approached to claim her hand, Charlotte could not help cautioning her in a whisper not to be a simpleton, and allow her fancy for Wickham to make her appear unpleasant in the eyes of a man of ten times his consequence.

Elizabeth made no answer, and took her place in the set, amazed at the dignity to which she was arrived in being allowed to stand opposite to Mr. Darcy, and reading in her neighbours' looks their equal amazement in beholding it. They stood for some time without speaking a word; and she began to imagine that their silence was to last through the two dances, and at first was resolved not to break it; till suddenly, fancying that it would be the greater punishment to her partner to oblige him to talk, she made some slight observation on the dance. He replied, and was again silent. After a pause of some minutes she addressed him a second time with—'It is *your* turn to say something now, Mr. Darcy. *I* talked about the dance, and *you* ought to make some kind of remark on the size of the room, or the number of couples.'

He smiled, and assured her that whatever she wished him to say should be said.

' Very well. That reply will do for the present. Perhaps by and by I may observe that private balls are much pleasanter than public ones. But *now* we may be silent.'

' Do you talk by rule, then, while you are dancing ? '

' Sometimes. One must speak a little, you know. It would look odd to be entirely silent for half an hour together ; and yet for the advantage of *some*, conversation ought to be so arranged, as that they may have the trouble of saying as little as possible.'

'Are you consulting your own feelings in the present case, or do you imagine that you are gratifying mine?'

'Both,' replied Elizabeth archly; 'for I have always seen a great similarity in the turn of our minds. We are each of an unsocial, taciturn disposition, unwilling to speak, unless we expect to say something that will amaze the whole room, and be handed down to posterity with all the *éclat* of a proverb.'

'This is no very striking resemblance of your own character, I am sure,' said he. 'How near it may be to *mine*, I cannot pretend to say. *You* think it a faithful portrait undoubtedly.'

'I must not decide on my own performance.'

He made no answer, and they were again silent till they had gone down the dance, when he asked her if she and her sisters did not very often walk to Meryton? She answered in the affirmative; and, unable to resist the temptation, added, 'When you met us there the other day, we had just been forming a new acquaintance.'

The effect was immediate. A deeper shade of hauteur overspread his features, but he said not a word, and Elizabeth, though blaming herself for her own weakness, could not go on. At length Darcy spoke, and in a constrained manner said, ' Mr. Wickham is blessed with such happy manners as may insure his *making* friends—whether he may be equally capable of *retaining* them, is less certain.'

'He has been so unlucky as to lose *your* friendship,' replied Elizabeth with emphasis, 'and in a manner which he is likely to suffer from all his life.'

Darcy made no answer, and seemed desirous of changing the subject. At that moment Sir William Lucas appeared close to them, meaning to pass through the set to the other side of the room; but on perceiving Mr. Darcy he stopped with a bow of superior courtesy to compliment him on his dancing and his partner.

'I have been most highly gratified indeed, my dear sir. Such very superior dancing is not often seen. It is evident that you belong to the first circles. Allow me to say, however, that your fair partner does not disgrace you, and that I must hope to have this pleasure often repeated, especially when a certain desirable event, my dear Miss Eliza (glancing at her sister and Bingley) shall take place. What congratulations will then flow in! I appeal to Mr. Darcy —but let me not interrupt you, sir. You will not thank me for detaining you from the bewitching converse of that young lady, whose bright eyes are also upbraiding me.'

The latter part of this address was scarcely heard by Darcy; but Sir William's allusion to his friend seemed to strike him forcibly, and his eyes were directed with a very serious expression towards Bingley and Jane, who were dancing together. Recovering himself, however, shortly, he turned to his partner, and said, 'Sir William's interruption has made me forget what we were talking of.'

'I do not think we were speaking at all. Sir William could not have interrupted any two people in the room who had less to say for themselves. We have tried two or three subjects already without success, and what we are to talk of next I cannot imagine.'

'What think you of books?' said he, smiling.

'Books—oh! no. I am sure we never read the same, or not with the same feelings.'

'I am sorry you think so; but if that be the case, there can at least be no want of subject. We may compare our different opinions.'

'No—I cannot talk of books in a ballroom; my head is always full of something else.'

'The *present* always occupies you in such scenes—does it?' said he, with a look of doubt.

'Yes, always,' she replied, without knowing what she said, for her thoughts had wandered

141

far from the subject, as soon afterwards appeared
by her suddenly exclaiming, ' I remember hearing you once say, Mr. Darcy, that you hardly
ever forgave, that your resentment once created
was unappeasable. You are very cautious, I
suppose, as to its *being created*.'

' I am,' said he, with a firm voice.

' And never allow yourself to be blinded by
prejudice ? '

' I hope not.'

' It is particularly incumbent on those who
never change their opinion, to be secure of
judging properly at first.'

' May I ask to what these questions tend ? '

' Merely to the illustration of *your* character,'
said she, endeavouring to shake off her gravity.
' I am trying to make it out.'

' And what is your success ? '

She shook her head. ' I do not get on at all.
I hear such different accounts of you as puzzle
me exceedingly.'

' I can readily believe,' answered he gravely,
' that reports may vary greatly with respect to
me ; and I could wish, Miss Bennet, that you
were not to sketch my character at the present
moment, as there is reason to fear that the performance would reflect no credit on either.'

' But if I do not take your likeness now, I
may never have another opportunity.'

142

'I would by no means suspend any pleasure of yours,' he coldly replied. She said no more, and they went down the other dance and parted in silence; on each side dissatisfied, though not to an equal degree, for in Darcy's breast there was a tolerable powerful feeling towards her, which soon procured her pardon, and directed all his anger against another.

They had not long separated when Miss Bingley came towards her, and with an expression of civil disdain thus accosted her :—'So, Miss Eliza, I hear you are quite delighted with George Wickham ! Your sister has been talking to me about him, and asking me a thousand questions ; and I find that the young man forgot to tell you, among his other communications, that he was the son of old Wickham, the late Mr. Darcy's steward. Let me recommend you, however, as a friend, not to give implicit confidence to all his assertions : for as to Mr. Darcy's using him ill, it is perfectly false ; for, on the contrary, he has been always remarkably kind to him, though George Wickham has treated Mr. Darcy in a most infamous manner. I do not know the particulars, but I know very well that Mr. Darcy is not in the least to blame, that he cannot bear to hear George Wickham mentioned, and that though my brother thought he could not well avoid including him in his invitation to the officers, he was excessively glad to find that he had taken himself out of the way. His coming into the country at all is a most insolent thing, indeed, and I wonder how he could presume to do it. I pity you, Miss Eliza, for this discovery of your favourite's guilt; but really, considering his descent, one could not expect much better.'

'His guilt and his descent appear by your account to be the same,' said Elizabeth angrily; 'for I have heard you accuse him of nothing worse than of being the son of Mr. Darcy's steward, and of *that*, I can assure you, he informed me himself.'

'I beg your pardon,' replied Miss Bingley, turning away with a sneer. 'Excuse my interference: it was kindly meant.'

'Insolent girl!' said Elizabeth to herself. 'You are much mistaken if you expect to influence me by such a paltry attack as this. I see nothing in it but your own wilful ignorance and the malice of Mr. Darcy.' She then sought her eldest sister, who had undertaken to make inquiries on the same subject of Bingley. Jane met her with a smile of such sweet complacency, a glow of such happy expression, as sufficiently marked how well she was satisfied with the occurrences of the evening. Elizabeth instantly read her feelings, and at that moment solicitude for Wickham, resentment against his enemies, and everything else, gave way before the hope of Jane's being in the fairest way for happiness.

'I want to know,' said she, with a countenance no less smiling than her sister's, 'what you have learnt about Mr. Wickham. But perhaps you have been too pleasantly engaged to think of any third person; in which case you may be sure of my pardon.'

'No,' replied Jane, 'I have not forgotten him; but I have nothing satisfactory to tell you. Mr. Bingley does not know the whole of his history, and is quite ignorant of the circumstances which have principally offended Mr. Darcy; but he will vouch for the good conduct, the probity, and honour of his friend, and is perfectly convinced that Mr. Wickham has deserved much less attention from Mr. Darcy than he has received; and I am sorry to say that by his account as well as his sister's, Mr. Wickham is by no means a respectable young man. I am afraid he has been very imprudent, and has deserved to lose Mr. Darcy's regard.'

'Mr. Bingley does not know Mr. Wickham himself?'

'No; he never saw him till the other morning at Meryton.'

'This account, then, is what he has received

from Mr. Darcy. I am perfectly satisfied. But what does he say of the living ? '

'He does not exactly recollect the circumstances, though he has heard them from Mr. Darcy more than once, but he believes that it was left to him *conditionally* only.'

'I have not a doubt of Mr. Bingley's sincerity,' said Elizabeth warmly ; 'but you must excuse my not being convinced by assurances only. Mr. Bingley's defence of his friend was a very able one, I dare say; but since he is unacquainted with several parts of the story, and has learnt the rest from that friend himself, I shall venture still to think of both gentlemen as I did before.'

She then changed the discourse to one more gratifying to each, and on which there could be no difference of sentiment. Elizabeth listened with delight to the happy, though modest hopes which Jane entertained of Bingley's regard, and said all in her power to heighten her confidence in it. On their being joined by Mr. Bingley himself, Elizabeth withdrew to Miss Lucas; to whose inquiry after the pleasantness of her last partner she had scarcely replied before Mr. Collins came up to them, and told her with great exultation that he had just been so fortunate as to make a most important discovery.

'I have found out,' said he, 'by a singular accident, that there is now in the room a near

relation of my patroness. I happened to overhear the gentleman himself mentioning to the
young lady who does the honours of this house
the names of his cousin Miss de Bourgh, and of
her mother Lady Catherine. How wonderfully
these sort of things occur! Who would have
thought of my meeting with, perhaps, a nephew
of Lady Catherine de Bourgh in this assembly!
I am most thankful that the discovery is made
in time for me to pay my respects to him, which
I am now going to do, and trust he will excuse
my not having done it before. My total
ignorance of the connexion must plead my
apology.'

'You are not going to introduce yourself to
Mr. Darcy!'

'Indeed I am. I shall entreat his pardon for
not having done it earlier. I believe him to be
Lady Catherine's *nephew*. It will be in my
power to assure him that her ladyship was quite
well yesterday se'nnight.'

Elizabeth tried hard to dissuade him from
such a scheme, assuring him that Mr. Darcy
would consider his addressing him without introduction as an impertinent freedom, rather
than a compliment to his aunt; that it was not
in the least necessary there should be any notice
on either side; and that if it were, it must
belong to Mr. Darcy, the superior in conse-

quence, to begin the acquaintance. Mr. Collins listened to her with the determined air of following his own inclination, and, when she ceased speaking, replied thus :—' My dear Miss Elizabeth, I have the highest opinion in the world of your excellent judgment in all matters within the scope of your understanding; but permit me to say that there must be a wide difference between the established forms of ceremony amongst the laity and those which regulate the clergy; for, give me leave to observe that I consider the clerical office as equal in point of dignity with the highest rank in the kingdom —provided that a proper humility of behaviour is at the same time maintained. You must, therefore, allow me to follow the dictates of my conscience on this occasion, which leads me to perform what I look on as a point of duty. Pardon me for neglecting to profit by your advice, which on every other subject shall be my constant guide, though in the case before us I consider myself more fitted by education and habitual study to decide on what is right than a young lady like yourself.' And with a low bow he left her to attack Mr. Darcy, whose reception of his advances she eagerly watched, and whose astonishment at being so addressed was very evident. Her cousin prefaced his speech with a solemn bow : and though

148

she could not hear a word of it, she felt as if hearing it all, and saw in the motion of his lips the words 'apology,' 'Hunsford,' and 'Lady Catherine de Bourgh.' It vexed her to see him expose himself to such a man. Mr. Darcy was eyeing him with unrestrained wonder, and when at last Mr. Collins allowed him time to speak, replied with an air of distant civility. Mr. Collins, however, was not discouraged from speaking again, and Mr. Darcy's contempt seemed abundantly increasing with the length of his second speech, and at the end of it he only made him a slight bow, and moved another way. Mr. Collins then returned to Elizabeth.

'I have no reason, I assure you,' said he, 'to be dissatisfied with my reception. Mr. Darcy seemed much pleased with the attention. He answered me with the utmost civility, and even paid me the compliment of saying that he was so well convinced of Lady Catherine's discernment as to be certain she could never bestow a favour unworthily. It was really a very handsome thought. Upon the whole, I am much pleased with him.'

As Elizabeth had no longer any interest of her own to pursue, she turned her attention almost entirely on her sister and Mr. Bingley; and the train of agreeable reflections which her observations gave birth to made her perhaps almost as happy as Jane. She saw her in idea settled in that very house, in all the felicity which a marriage of true affection could bestow; and she felt capable, under such circumstances, of endeavouring even to like Bingley's two sisters. Her mother's thoughts she plainly saw were bent the same way, and she determined not to venture near her, lest she might hear too much. When they sat down to supper, therefore, she considered it a most unlucky perverseness which placed them within one of each other; and deeply was she vexed to find that her mother was talking to that one person (Lady Lucas) freely, openly, and of nothing else but of her expectation that Jane would be soon married to Mr. Bingley.—It was an animating subject, and Mrs. Bennet seemed incapable of fatigue while enumerating the advantages of the match. His being such a charming young man, and so rich, and living but three miles from them, were the first points of self-gratulation; and then it was such a comfort to think how fond the two sisters were of Jane, and to be certain that they must desire the connexion as much as she could do. It was, moreover, such a promising thing for her younger daughters, as Jane's marrying so greatly must throw them in the way of other rich men; and lastly, it was so pleasant at her time of life to be able to consign her single daughters to the care of their sister, that she might not be obliged to go into company more than she liked. It was necessary to make this circumstance a matter of pleasure, because on such occasions it is the etiquette; but no one was less likely than Mrs. Bennet to find comfort in staying at home at any period of her life. She concluded with many good wishes that Lady Lucas might soon be equally fortunate, though evidently and triumphantly believing there was no chance of it.

In vain did Elizabeth endeavour to check the rapidity of her mother's words, or persuade her to describe her felicity in a less audible whisper; for, to her inexpressible vexation, she could perceive that the chief of it was overheard by Mr. Darcy, who sat opposite to them. Her mother only scolded her for being nonsensical.

'What is Mr. Darcy to me, pray, that I should be afraid of him? I am sure we owe him no such particular civility as to be obliged to say nothing *he* may not like to hear.'

'For Heaven's sake, madam, speak lower.— What advantage can it be to you to offend Mr. Darcy? You will never recommend yourself to his friend by so doing.'

Nothing that she could say, however, had any influence. Her mother would talk of her views in the same intelligible tone. Elizabeth blushed

and blushed again with shame and vexation.
She could not help frequently glancing her eye
at Mr. Darcy, though every glance convinced
her of what she dreaded; for though he was not
always looking at her mother, she was convinced
that his attention was invariably fixed by her.
The expression of his face changed gradually
from indignant contempt to a composed and
steady gravity.

At length, however, Mrs. Bennet had no
more to say; and Lady Lucas, who had been
long yawning at the repetition of delights which
she saw no likelihood of sharing, was left to the
comforts of cold ham and chicken. Elizabeth
now began to revive.   But not long was the
interval of tranquillity; for, when supper was
over, singing was talked of, and she had the
mortification of seeing Mary, after very little
entreaty, preparing to oblige the company. By
many significant looks and silent entreaties did
she endeavour to prevent such a proof of complaisance—but in vain: Mary would not understand them; such an opportunity of exhibiting
was delightful to her, and she began her song.
Elizabeth's eyes were fixed on her with most
painful sensations, and she watched her progress
through the several stanzas with an impatience
which was very ill rewarded at their close; for
Mary, on receiving, amongst the thanks of the

table, the hint of a hope that she might be prevailed on to favour them again, after the pause
of half a minute began another. Mary's powers
were by no means fitted for such a display : her
voice was weak, and her manner affected.—
Elizabeth was in agonies. She looked at Jane,
to see how she bore it ; but Jane was very
composedly talking to Bingley. She looked at
his two sisters, and saw them making signs of
derision at each other, and at Darcy, who
continued, however, impenetrably grave. She
looked at her father to entreat his interference,
lest Mary should be singing all night. He took
the hint, and when Mary had finished her second
song, said aloud, 'That will do extremely well,
child. You have delighted us long enough.
Let the other young ladies have time to exhibit.'

Mary, though pretending not to hear, was
somewhat disconcerted ; and Elizabeth, sorry
for her, and sorry for her father's speech, was
afraid her anxiety had done no good. Others
of the party were now applied to.

'If I,' said Mr. Collins, 'were so fortunate as
to be able to sing, I should have great pleasure,
I am sure, in obliging the company with an air ;
for I consider music as a very innocent diversion,
and perfectly compatible with the profession of
a clergyman.—I do not mean, however, to assert
that we can be justified in devoting too much of

our time to music, for there are certainly other
things to be attended to. The rector of a parish
has much to do.—In the first place, he must
make such an agreement for tithes as may be
beneficial to himself and not offensive to his
patron. He must write his own sermons; and
the time that remains will not be too much for
his parish duties, and the care and improvement
of his dwelling, which he cannot be excused from
making as comfortable as possible. And I do
not think it of light importance that he should
have attentive and conciliatory manners towards
everybody, especially towards those to whom he
owes his preferment. I cannot acquit him of
that duty; nor could I think well of the man
who should omit an occasion of testifying his
respect towards anybody connected with the
family.' And with a bow to Mr. Darcy he
concluded his speech, which had been spoken so
loud as to be heard by half the room.—Many
stared—many smiled; but no one looked more
amused that Mr. Bennet himself, while his wife
seriously commended Mr. Collins for having
spoken so sensibly, and observed in a half-
whisper to Lady Lucas, that he was a remarkably clever, good kind of young man.

To Elizabeth it appeared that had her family
made an agreement to expose themselves as
much as they could during the evening, it would

154

have been impossible for them to play their parts
with more spirit or finer success; and happy did
she think it for Bingley and her sister that some
of the exhibition had escaped his notice, and
that his feelings were not of a sort to be much
distressed by the folly which he must have
witnessed. That his two sisters and Mr. Darcy,
however, should have such an opportunity of
ridiculing her relations, was bad enough, and she
could not determine whether the silent contempt of the gentleman, or the insolent smiles
of the ladies, were more intolerable.

The rest of the evening brought her little
amusement. She was teased by Mr. Collins,
who continued most perseveringly by her side,
and though he could not prevail with her to
dance with him again, put it out of her power
to dance with others. In vain did she entreat
him to stand up with somebody else, and offer
to introduce him to any young lady in the room.
He assured her that, as to dancing, he was perfectly indifferent to it; that his chief object was,
by delicate attentions, to recommend himself to
her, and that he should therefore make a point
of remaining close to her the whole evening.
There was no arguing upon such a project. She
owed her greatest relief to her friend Miss Lucas,
who often joined them, and good-naturedly
engaged Mr. Collins's conversation to herself.

She was at least free from the offence of Mr. Darcy's farther notice; though often standing within a very short distance of her, quite disengaged, he never came near enough to speak. She felt it to be the probable consequence of her allusions to Mr. Wickham, and rejoiced in it.

The Longbourn party were the last of all the company to depart, and, by a manœuvre of Mrs. Bennet, had to wait for their carriage a quarter of an hour after everybody else was gone, which gave them time to see how heartily they were wished away by some of the family. Mrs. Hurst and her sister scarcely opened their mouths, except to complain of fatigue, and were evidently impatient to have the house to themselves. They repulsed every attempt of Mrs. Bennet at conversation, and by so doing threw a languor over the whole party, which was very little relieved by the long speeches of Mr. Collins, who was complimenting Mr. Bingley and his sisters on the elegance of their entertainment, and the hospitality and politeness which had marked their behaviour to their guests. Darcy said nothing at all. Mr. Bennet, in equal silence, was enjoying the scene. Mr. Bingley and Jane were standing together, a little detached from the rest, and talked only to each other. Elizabeth preserved as steady a silence as either Mrs. Hurst or Miss Bingley; and even

Lydia was too much fatigued to utter more than the occasional exclamation of 'Lord, how tired I am!' accompanied by a violent yawn.

When at length they arose to take leave, Mrs. Bennet was most pressingly civil in her hope of seeing the whole family soon at Longbourn, and addressed herself particularly to Mr. Bingley, to assure him how happy he would make them by eating a family dinner with them at any time, without the ceremony of a formal invitation. Bingley was all grateful pleasure, and he readily engaged for taking the earliest opportunity of waiting on her after his return from London, whither he was obliged to go the next day for a short time.

Mrs. Bennet was perfectly satisfied, and quitted the house under the delightful persuasion that, allowing for the necessary preparations of settlements, new carriages, and wedding-clothes, she should undoubtedly see her daughter settled at Netherfield in the course of three or four months. Of having another daughter married to Mr. Collins, she thought with equal certainty, and with considerable, though not equal, pleasure. Elizabeth was the least dear to her of all her children; and though the man and the match were quite good enough for *her*, the worth of each was eclipsed by Mr. Bingley and Netherfield.

CHAPTER XIX

THE next day opened a new scene at Longbourn. Mr. Collins made his declaration in form.
Having resolved to do it without loss of time,
as his leave of absence extended only to the
following Saturday, and having no feelings of
diffidence to make it distressing to himself even
at the moment, he set about it in a very orderly
manner, with all the observances which he supposed a regular part of the business. On finding
Mrs. Bennet, Elizabeth, and one of the younger
girls together, soon after breakfast, he addressed
the mother in these words: 'May I hope, madam,
for your interest with your fair daughter Elizabeth, when I solicit for the honour of a private
audience with her in the course of this morning?'

Before Elizabeth had time for anything but a
blush of surprise, Mrs. Bennet instantly answered,
'Oh dear! Yes—certainly. I am sure Lizzy
will be very happy—I am sure she can have no
objection. Come, Kitty, I want you upstairs.'
And gathering her work together, she was
hastening away, when Elizabeth called out—

158

'Dear ma'am, do not go. I beg you will not go. Mr. Collins must excuse me. He can have nothing to say to me that anybody need not hear. I am going away myself.'

'No, no, nonsense, Lizzy. I desire you will stay where you are.' And upon Elizabeth's seeming really, with vexed and embarrassed looks, about to escape, she added, 'Lizzy, I *insist* upon your staying and hearing Mr. Collins.'

Elizabeth would not oppose such an injunction —and a moment's consideration making her also sensible that it would be wisest to get it over as soon and as quietly as possible, she sat down again, and tried to conceal, by incessant employment, the feelings which were divided between distress and diversion. Mrs. Bennet and Kitty walked off, and as soon as they were gone Mr. Collins began.

'Believe me, my dear Miss Elizabeth, that your modesty, so far from doing you any disservice, rather adds to your other perfections. You would have been less amiable in my eyes had there *not* been this little unwillingness; but allow me to assure you, that I have your respected mother's permission for this address. You can hardly doubt the purport of my discourse, however your natural delicacy may lead you to dissemble; my attentions have been too marked to be mistaken. Almost as soon as I entered the house, I singled you out as the companion of my future life. But before I am run away with by my feelings on this subject, perhaps it would be advisable for me to state my reasons for marrying—and, moreover, for coming into Hertfordshire with the design of selecting a wife, as I certainly did.'

The idea of Mr. Collins, with all his solemn composure, being run away with by his feelings, made Elizabeth so near laughing that she could not use the short pause he allowed in any attempt to stop him farther, and he continued—

'My reasons for marrying are, first, that I think it a right thing for every clergyman in easy circumstances (like myself) to set the example of matrimony in his parish; secondly, that I am convinced it will add very greatly to my happiness; and thirdly—which perhaps I ought to have mentioned earlier, that it is the particular advice and recommendation of the very noble lady whom I have the honour of calling patroness. Twice has she condescended to give me her opinion (unasked too!) on this subject; and it was but the very Saturday night before I left Hunsford—between our pools at quadrille, while Mrs. Jenkinson was arranging Miss de Bourgh's footstool—that she said, "Mr. Collins, you must marry. A clergyman like you must marry. — Chuse properly, chuse a gentlewoman for *my* sake; and for your *own*, let her be an active, useful sort of person, not brought up high, but able to make a small income go a good way. This is my advice. Find such a woman as soon as you can, bring her to Hunsford, and I will visit her." Allow me, by the way, to observe, my fair cousin, that I do not reckon the notice and kindness of Lady Catherine de Bourgh as among the least of the advantages in my power to offer. You will find her manners beyond anything I can describe; and your wit and vivacity, I think, must be acceptable to her, especially when tempered with the silence and respect which her rank will inevitably excite. Thus much for my general intention in favour of matrimony; it remains to be told why my views were directed to Longbourn instead of my own neighbourhood, where, I assure you, there are many amiable young women. But the fact is, that being, as I am, to inherit this estate after the death of your honoured father (who, however, may live many years longer), I could not satisfy myself without resolving to chuse a wife from among his daughters, that the loss to them might be as little as possible, when the melancholy event takes place—which, however, as I have already said, may not be for several years.

This has been my motive, my fair cousin, and I flatter myself it will not sink me in your esteem. And now nothing remains for me but to assure you in the most animated language of the violence of my affection. To fortune I am perfectly indifferent, and shall make no demand of that nature on your father, since I am well aware that it could not be complied with; and that one thousand pounds in the four per cents., which will not be yours till after your mother's decease, is all that you may ever be entitled to. On that head, therefore, I shall be uniformly silent; and you may assure yourself that no ungenerous reproach shall ever pass my lips when we are married.'

It was absolutely necessary to interrupt him now.

'You are too hasty, sir,' she cried. 'You forget that I have made no answer. Let me do it without farther loss of time. Accept my thanks for the compliment you are paying me. I am very sensible of the honour of your proposals, but it is impossible for me to do otherwise than decline them.'

'I am not now to learn,' replied Mr. Collins, with a formal wave of the hand, 'that it is usual with young ladies to reject the addresses of the man whom they secretly mean to accept, when he first applies for their favour; and that sometimes the refusal is repeated a second or even a third time. I am therefore by no means discouraged by what you have just said, and shall hope to lead you to the altar ere long.'

'Upon my word, sir,' cried Elizabeth, 'your hope is rather an extraordinary one after my declaration. I do assure you that I am not one of those young ladies (if such young ladies there are) who are so daring as to risk their happiness on the chance of being asked a second time. I am perfectly serious in my refusal. You could not make *me* happy, and I am convinced that I am the last woman in the world who would make *you* so. Nay, were your friend Lady Catherine to know me, I am persuaded she would find me in every respect ill qualified for the situation.'

'Were it certain that Lady Catherine would think so,' said Mr. Collins very gravely—' but I cannot imagine that her ladyship would at all disapprove of you. And you may be certain that when I have the honour of seeing her again, I shall speak in the highest terms of your modesty, economy, and other amiable qualifications.'

'Indeed, Mr. Collins, all praise of me will be unnecessary. You must give me leave to judge for myself, and pay me the compliment of be-

lieving what I say. I wish you very happy and
very rich, and by refusing your hand, do all in
my power to prevent your being otherwise. In
making me the offer, you must have satisfied
the delicacy of your feelings with regard to my
family, and may take possession of Longbourn
estate whenever it falls, without any self-re-
proach. This matter may be considered, therefore, as finally settled.' And rising as she thus
spoke, she would have quitted the room, had
not Mr. Collins thus addressed her—

'When I do myself the honour of speaking
to you next on the subject, I shall hope to receive a more favourable answer than you have
now given me ; though I am far from accusing
you of cruelty at present, because I know it to
be the established custom of your sex to reject
a man on the first application, and perhaps you
have even now said as much to encourage
my suit as would be consistent with the true
delicacy of the female character.'

'Really, Mr. Collins,' cried Elizabeth with
some warmth, 'you puzzle me exceedingly. If
what I have hitherto said can appear to you in
the form of encouragement, I know not how to
express my refusal in such a way as may convince you of its being one.'

'You must give me leave to flatter myself,
my dear cousin, that your refusal of my addresses

is merely words of course. My reasons for believing it are briefly these :—It does not appear
to me that my hand is unworthy your acceptance, or that the establishment I can offer would
be any other than highly desirable. My situation in life, my connexions with the family of
De Bourgh, and my relationship to your own,
are circumstances highly in my favour; and you
should take it into farther consideration that,
in spite of your manifold attractions, it is by no
means certain that another offer of marriage may
ever be made you. Your portion is unhappily
so small, that it will in all likelihood undo the
effects of your loveliness and amiable qualifications. As I must therefore conclude that you
are not serious in your rejection of me, I shall
chuse to attribute it to your wish of increasing
my love by suspense, according to the usual
practice of elegant females.'

‘I do assure you, sir, that I have no pretensions whatever to that kind of elegance which
consists in tormenting a respectable man. I
would rather be paid the compliment of being
believed sincere. I thank you again and again
for the honour you have done me in your proposals, but to accept them is absolutely impossible. My feelings in every respect forbid it.
Can I speak plainer? Do not consider me now
as an elegant female, intending to plague you,

but as a rational creature, speaking the truth from her heart.'

'You are uniformly charming!' cried he, with an air of awkward gallantry; 'and I am persuaded that, when sanctioned by the express authority of both your excellent parents, my proposals will not fail of being acceptable.'

To such perseverance in wilful self-deception Elizabeth would make no reply, and immediately and in silence withdrew; determined, that if he persisted in considering her repeated refusals as flattering encouragement, to apply to her father, whose negative might be uttered in such a manner as must be decisive, and whose behaviour at least could not be mistaken for the affectation and coquetry of an elegant female.

CHAPTER XX

MR. COLLINS was not left long to the silent
contemplation of his successful love; for Mrs.
Bennet, having dawdled about in the vestibule
to watch for the end of the conference, no sooner
saw Elizabeth open the door and with quick
step pass her towards the staircase, than she
entered the breakfast-room, and congratulated
both him and herself in warm terms on the
happy prospect of their nearer connexion. Mr.
Collins received and returned these felicitations
with equal pleasure, and then proceeded to relate
the particulars of their interview, with the result
of which he trusted he had every reason to be
satisfied, since the refusal which his cousin had
steadfastly given him would naturally flow from
her bashful modesty and the genuine delicacy
of her character.

This information, however, startled Mrs.
Bennet; she would have been glad to be equally
satisfied that her daughter had meant to encourage him by protesting against his proposals,

but she dared not believe it, and could not help saying so.

'But, depend upon it, Mr. Collins,' she added, 'that Lizzy shall be brought to reason. I will speak to her about it myself directly. She is a very headstrong, foolish girl, and does not know her own interest; but I will *make* her know it.'

'Pardon me for interrupting you, madam,' cried Mr. Collins; 'but if she is really headstrong and foolish, I know not whether she would altogether be a very desirable wife to a man in my situation, who naturally looks for happiness in the marriage state. If, therefore, she actually persists in rejecting my suit, perhaps it were better not to force her into accepting me, because if liable to such defects of temper, she could not contribute much to my felicity.'

'Sir, you quite misunderstand me,' said Mrs. Bennet, alarmed. 'Lizzy is only headstrong in such matters as these. In everything else she is as good-natured a girl as ever lived. I will go directly to Mr. Bennet, and we shall very soon settle it with her, I am sure.'

She would not give him time to reply, but hurrying instantly to her husband, called out as she entered the library, 'Oh! Mr. Bennet, you are wanted immediately; we are all in an up-roar. You must come and make Lizzy marry

Mr. Collins, for she vows she will not have him, and if you do not make haste he will change his mind and not have *her*.'

Mr. Bennet raised his eyes from his book as she entered, and fixed them on her face with a calm unconcern which was not in the least altered by her communication.

'I have not the pleasure of understanding you,' said he, when she had finished her speech. 'Of what are you talking?'

'Of Mr. Collins and Lizzy. Lizzy declares she will not have Mr. Collins, and Mr. Collins begins to say that he will not have Lizzy.'

'And what am I to do on the occasion?—It seems an hopeless business.'

'Speak to Lizzy about it yourself. Tell her that you insist upon her marrying him.'

'Let her be called down. She shall hear my opinion.'

Mrs. Bennet rang the bell, and Miss Elizabeth was summoned to the library.

'Come here, child,' cried her father as she appeared. 'I have sent for you on an affair of importance. I understand that Mr. Collins has made you an offer of marriage. Is it true?' Elizabeth replied that it was. 'Very well— and this offer of marriage you have refused?'

'I have, sir.'

'Very well. We now come to the point.

169

Your mother insists upon your accepting it. Is it not so, Mrs. Bennet?'

'Yes, or I will never see her again.'

'An unhappy alternative is before you, Elizabeth. From this day you must be a stranger to one of your parents. Your mother will never see you again if you do *not* marry Mr. Collins, and I will never see you again if you *do*.'

Elizabeth could not but smile at such a conclusion of such a beginning; but Mrs. Bennet, who had persuaded herself that her husband regarded the affair as she wished, was excessively disappointed.

'What do you mean, Mr. Bennet, by talking in this way? You promised me to *insist* upon her marrying him.'

'My dear,' replied her husband, 'I have two small favours to request. First, that you will allow me the free use of my understanding on the present occasion; and secondly, of my room. I shall be glad to have the library to myself as soon as may be.'

Not yet, however, in spite of her disappointment in her husband, did Mrs. Bennet give up the point. She talked to Elizabeth again and again; coaxed and threatened her by turns. She endeavoured to secure Jane in her interest; but Jane, with all possible mildness, declined interfering; and Elizabeth, sometimes with real

170

earnestness, and sometimes with playful gaiety, replied to her attacks. Though her manner varied, however, her determination never did.

Mr. Collins, meanwhile, was meditating in solitude on what had passed. He thought too well of himself to comprehend on what motive his cousin could refuse him; and though his pride was hurt, he suffered in no other way. His regard for her was quite imaginary; and the possibility of her deserving her mother's reproach prevented his feeling any regret.

While the family were in this confusion, Charlotte Lucas came to spend the day with them. She was met in the vestibule by Lydia, who, flying to her, cried in a half-whisper, 'I am glad you are come, for there is such fun here! What do you think has happened this morning? —Mr. Collins has made an offer to Lizzy, and she will not have him.'

Charlotte had hardly time to answer before they were joined by Kitty, who came to tell the same news; and no sooner had they entered the breakfast-room, where Mrs. Bennet was alone, then she likewise began on the subject, calling on Miss Lucas for her compassion, and entreating her to persuade her friend Lizzy to comply with the wishes of all her family. 'Pray do, my dear Miss Lucas,' she added in a melancholy tone, 'for nobody is on my side, nobody takes

171

part with me; I am cruelly used, nobody feels
for my poor nerves.'

Charlotte's reply was spared by the entrance
of Jane and Elizabeth.

'Ay, there she comes,' continued Mrs. Bennet, 'looking as unconcerned as may be, and
caring no more for us than if we were at York,
provided she can have her own way. But I tell
you what, Miss Lizzy—if you take it into your
head to go on refusing every offer of marriage
in this way, you will never get an husband at all
—and I am sure I do not know who is to main-
tain you when your father is dead. *I* shall not
be able to keep you—and so I warn you. I
have done with you from this very day. I told
you in the library, you know, that I should
never speak to you again, and you will find me
as good as my word. I have no pleasure in
talking to undutiful children. Not that I have
much pleasure, indeed, in talking to anybody.
People who suffer as I do from nervous complaints can have no great inclination for talking.
Nobody can tell what I suffer! But it is always
so. Those who do not complain are never
pitied.'

Her daughters listened in silence to this
effusion, sensible that any attempt to reason
with or soothe her would only increase the
irritation. She talked on, therefore, without

172

interruption from any of them, till they were joined by Mr. Collins, who entered with an air more stately than usual, and on perceiving whom she said to the girls, 'Now, I do insist upon it, that you, all of you hold your tongues, and let Mr. Collins and me have a little conversation together.'

Elizabeth passed quietly out of the room, Jane and Kitty followed, but Lydia stood her ground, determined to hear all she could; and Charlotte, detained first by the civility of Mr. Collins, whose inquiries after herself and all her family were very minute, and then by a little curiosity, satisfied herself with walking to the window and pretending not to hear. In a doleful voice Mrs. Bennet thus began the projected conversation :—
'Oh ! Mr. Collins !'

'My dear madam,' replied he, 'let us be for ever silent on this point. Far be it from me,' he presently continued, in a voice that marked his displeasure, 'to resent the behaviour of your daughter. Resignation to inevitable evils is the duty of us all; the peculiar duty of a young man who has been so fortunate as I have been in early preferment; and I trust I am resigned. Perhaps not the less so from feeling a doubt of my positive happiness had my fair cousin honoured me with her hand; for I have often observed that resignation is never so perfect as

when the blessing denied begins to lose somewhat of its value in our estimation. You will
not, I hope, consider me as shewing any disrespect to your family, my dear madam, by thus
withdrawing my pretensions to your daughter's
favour, without having paid yourself and Mr.
Bennet the compliment of requesting you to
interpose your authority in my behalf. My
conduct may, I fear, be objectionable in having
accepted my dismission from your daughter's
lips instead of your own. But we are all liable
to error. I have certainly meant well through
the whole affair. My object has been to secure
an amiable companion for myself, with due consideration for the advantage of all your family,
and if my *manner* has been at all reprehensible,
I here beg leave to apologise.'

CHAPTER XXI

THE discussion of Mr. Collins's offer was now
nearly at an end, and Elizabeth had only to
suffer from the uncomfortable feelings necessarily
attending it, and occasionally from some peevish
allusion of her mother. As for the gentleman
himself, *his* feelings were chiefly expressed, not
by embarrassment or dejection, or by trying
to avoid her, but by stiffness of manner and
resentful silence. He scarcely ever spoke to her,
and the assiduous attentions which he had been
so sensible of himself were transferred for the
rest of the day to Miss Lucas, whose civility in
listening to him was a seasonable relief to them
all, and especially to her friend.

The morrow produced no abatement of Mrs.
Bennet's ill-humour or ill-health. Mr. Collins
was also in the same state of angry pride. Elizabeth had hoped that his resentment might
shorten his visit, but his plan did not appear
in the least affected by it. He was always to
have gone on Saturday, and to Saturday he still
meant to stay.

After breakfast the girls walked to Meryton, to inquire if Mr. Wickham were returned, and to lament over his absence from the Netherfield ball. He joined them on their entering the town, and attended them to their aunt's, where his regret and vexation, and the concern of everybody, were well talked over.—To Elizabeth, however, he voluntarily acknowledged that the necessity of his absence *had* been self-imposed.

'I found,' said he, 'as the time drew near, that I had better not meet Mr. Darcy;—that to be in the same room, the same party with him for so many hours together, might be more than I could bear, and that scenes might arise unpleasant to more than myself.'

She highly approved his forbearance, and they had leisure for a full discussion of it, and for all the commendation which they civilly bestowed on each other, as Wickham and another officer walked back with them to Longbourn, and during the walk he particularly attended to her. His accompanying them was a double advantage; she felt all the compliment it offered to herself, and it was most acceptable as an occasion of introducing him to her father and mother.

Soon after their return a letter was delivered to Miss Bennet; it came from Netherfield, and was opened immediately. The envelope contained a sheet of elegant, little, hot-pressed

176

paper, well covered with a lady's fair, flowing hand; and Elizabeth saw her sister's countenance change as she read it, and saw her dwelling intently on some particular passages. Jane recollected herself soon, and putting the letter away, tried to join with her usual cheerfulness in the general conversation; but Elizabeth felt an anxiety on the subject, which drew off her attention even from Wickham; and no sooner had he and his companion taken leave than a glance from Jane invited her to follow her upstairs. When they had gained their own room, Jane, taking out her letter, said, 'This is from Caroline Bingley; what it contains has surprised me a good deal. The whole party have left Netherfield by this time, and are on their way to town—and without any intention of coming back again. You shall hear what she says.'

She then read the first sentence aloud, which comprised the information of their having just resolved to follow their brother to town directly, and of their meaning to dine that day in Grosvenor Street, where Mr. Hurst had an house. The next was in these words: 'I do not pretend to regret anything I shall leave in Hertfordshire except your society, my dearest friend; but we will hope, at some future period, to enjoy many returns of that delightful intercourse we have known, and in the meanwhile may lessen the

3 M   177

pain of separation by a very frequent and most unreserved correspondence. I depend on you for that.' To these high-flown expressions Elizabeth listened with all the insensibility of distrust; and though the suddenness of their removal surprised her, she saw nothing in it really to lament : it was not to be supposed that their absence from Netherfield would prevent Mr. Bingley's being there ; and as to the loss of their society, she was persuaded that Jane must soon cease to regard it, in the enjoyment of his.

'It is unlucky,' said she, after a short pause, 'that you should not be able to see your friends before they leave the country. But may we not hope that the period of future happiness to which Miss Bingley looks forward may arrive earlier than she is aware, and that the delightful intercourse you have known as friends will be renewed with yet greater satisfaction as sisters ? Mr. Bingley will not be detained in London by them.'

'Caroline decidedly says that none of the party will return into Hertfordshire this winter. I will read it to you.

'"When my brother left us yesterday, he imagined that the business which took him to London might be concluded in three or four days; but as we are certain it cannot be so, and at the same time convinced that when Charles

gets to town he will be in no hurry to leave it
again, we have determined on following him
thither, that he may not be obliged to spend
his vacant hours in a comfortless hotel. Many
of my acquaintance are already there for the
winter; I wish I could hear that you, my
dearest friend, had any intention of making one
in the crowd—but of that I despair. I sincerely
hope your Christmas in Hertfordshire may
abound in the gaieties which that season generally brings, and that your beaux will be so
numerous as to prevent your feeling the loss
of the three of whom we shall deprive you."'

'It is evident by this,' added Jane, 'that he
comes back no more this winter.'

'It is only evident that Miss Bingley does
not mean he *should*.'

'Why will you think so? It must be his
own doing. He is his own master. But you
do not know *all*. I *will* read you the passage
which particularly hurts me. I will have no
reserves from *you*.

'"Mr. Darcy is impatient to see his sister;
and, to confess the truth, *we* are scarcely less
eager to meet her again. I really do not think
Georgiana Darcy has her equal for beauty,
elegance, and accomplishments; and the affection she inspires in Louisa and myself is heightened into something still more interesting, from

179

the hope we dare to entertain of her being hereafter our sister. I do not know whether I ever before mentioned to you my feelings on this subject; but I will not leave the country without confiding them, and I trust you will not esteem them unreasonable. My brother admires her greatly already; he will have frequent opportunity now of seeing her on the most intimate footing; her relations all wish the connexion as much as his own; and a sister's partiality is not misleading me, I think, when I call Charles most capable of engaging any woman's heart. With all these circumstances to favour an attachment, and nothing to prevent it, am I wrong, my dearest Jane, in indulging the hope of an event which will secure the happiness of so many?'

'What think you of *this* sentence, my dear Lizzy?' said Jane, as she finished it. 'Is it not clear enough? Does it not expressly declare that Caroline neither expects nor wishes me to be her sister; that she is perfectly convinced of her brother's indifference; and that if she suspects the nature of my feelings for him, she means (most kindly!) to put me on my guard? Can there be any other opinion on the subject?'

'Yes, there can; for mine is totally different. Will you hear it?'

'Most willingly.'

180

'You shall have it in a few words. Miss Bingley sees that her brother is in love with you, and wants him to marry Miss Darcy. She follows him to town in the hope of keeping him there, and tries to persuade you that he does not care about you.'

Jane shook her head.

'Indeed, Jane, you ought to believe me. No one who has ever seen you together can doubt his affection. Miss Bingley, I am sure, cannot. She is not such a simpleton. Could she have seen half as much love in Mr. Darcy for herself, she would have ordered her wedding-clothes. But the case is this :—We are not rich enough or grand enough for them ; and she is the more anxious to get Miss Darcy for her brother, from the notion that when there has been *one* inter-marriage, she may have less trouble in achieving a second ; in which there is certainly some in-genuity, and I dare say it would succeed if Miss de Bourgh were out of the way. But, my dearest Jane, you cannot seriously imagine that because Miss Bingley tells you her brother greatly admires Miss Darcy, he is in the smallest degree less sensible of *your* merit than when he took leave of you on Tuesday, or that it will be in her power to persuade him that, instead of being in love with you, he is very much in love with her friend.'

3 M*   181

' If we thought alike of Miss Bingley,' replied Jane, 'your representation of all this might make me quite easy. But I know the foundation is unjust. Caroline is incapable of wilfully deceiving any one; and all that I can hope in this case is that she is deceived herself.'

'That is right. You could not have started a more happy idea, since you will not take comfort in mine. Believe her to be deceived, by all means. You have now done your duty by her, and must fret no longer.'

'But, my dear sister, can I be happy, even supposing the best, in accepting a man whose sisters and friends are all wishing him to marry elsewhere ? '

'You must decide for yourself,' said Elizabeth ; 'and if, upon mature deliberation, you find that the misery of disobliging his two sisters is more than equivalent to the happiness of being his wife, I advise you by all means to refuse him.'

'How can you talk so ? ' said Jane, faintly smiling. 'You must know that though I should be exceedingly grieved at their disapprobation, I could not hesitate.'

'I did not think you would : and that being the case, I cannot consider your situation with much compassion.'

' But if he returns no more this winter, my choice will never be required. A thousand things may arise in six months ! '

The idea of his returning no more Elizabeth treated with the utmost contempt. It appeared to her merely the suggestion of Caroline's interested wishes, and she could not for a moment suppose that those wishes, however openly or artfully spoken, could influence a young man so totally independent of every one.

She represented to her sister as forcibly as possible what she felt on the subject, and had soon the pleasure of seeing its happy effect. Jane's temper was not desponding, and she was gradually led to hope, though the diffidence of affection sometimes overcame the hope, that Bingley would return to Netherfield and answer every wish of her heart.

They agreed that Mrs. Bennet should only hear of the departure of the family, without being alarmed on the score of the gentleman's conduct; but even this partial communication gave her a great deal of concern, and she bewailed it as exceedingly unlucky that the ladies should happen to go away just as they were all getting so intimate together. After lamenting it, however, at some length, she had the consolation of thinking that Mr. Bingley would be

soon down again and soon dining at Longbourn ;
and the conclusion of all was the comfortable
declaration that, though he had been invited
only to a family dinner, she would take care to
have two full courses.

CHAPTER XXII

THE Bennets were engaged to dine with the Lucases, and again during the chief of the day was Miss Lucas so kind as to listen to Mr. Collins. Elizabeth took an opportunity of thanking her. 'It keeps him in good humour,' said she, 'and I am more obliged to you than I can express.' Charlotte assured her friend of her satisfaction in being useful, and that it amply repaid her for the little sacrifice of her time. This was very amiable, but Charlotte's kindness extended farther than Elizabeth had any conception of;—its object was nothing else than to secure her from any return of Mr. Collins's addresses, by engaging them towards herself. Such was Miss Lucas's scheme; and appearances were so favourable, that when they parted at night she would have felt almost sure of success if he had not been to leave Hertfordshire so very soon. But here she did injustice to the fire and independence of his character, for it led him to escape out of Longbourn House the next morning with admirable slyness, and hasten to Lucas Lodge to throw himself at her feet. He was anxious to avoid the notice of his cousins, from a conviction that if they saw him depart, they could not fail to conjecture his design, and he was not willing to have the attempt known till its success could be known likewise; for though feeling almost secure, and with reason, for Charlotte had been tolerably encouraging, he was comparatively diffident since the adventure of Wednesday. His reception, however, was of the most flattering kind. Miss Lucas perceived him from an upper window as he walked towards the house, and instantly set out to meet him accidentally in the lane. But little had she dared to hope that so much love and eloquence awaited her there.

In as short a time as Mr. Collins's long speeches would allow, everything was settled between them to the satisfaction of both; and as they entered the house he earnestly entreated her to name the day that was to make him the happiest of men; and though such a solicitation must be waived for the present, the lady felt no inclination to trifle with his happiness. The stupidity with which he was favoured by nature must guard his courtship from any charm that could make a woman wish for its continuance; and Miss Lucas, who accepted him solely from the pure and disinterested desire of an establish-

ment, cared not how soon that establishment
were gained.

Sir William and Lady Lucas were speedily
applied to for their consent; and it was bestowed
with a most joyful alacrity. Mr. Collins's present
circumstances made it a most eligible match for
their daughter, to whom they could give little
fortune; and his prospects of future wealth were
exceedingly fair. Lady Lucas began directly
to calculate, with more interest than the matter
had ever excited before, how many years longer
Mr. Bennet was likely to live; and Sir William
gave it as his decided opinion that, whenever
Mr. Collins should be in possession of the Longbourn estate, it would be highly expedient that
both he and his wife should make their appearance at St. James's. The whole family, in short,
were properly overjoyed on the occasion. The
younger girls formed hopes of *coming out* a year
or two sooner than they might otherwise have
done; and the boys were relieved from their
apprehension of Charlotte's dying an old maid.
Charlotte herself was tolerably composed. She
had gained her point, and had time to consider
of it. Her reflections were in general satisfactory.
Mr. Collins, to be sure, was neither sensible
nor agreeable; his society was irksome, and his
attachment to her must be imaginary. But still
he would be her husband. Without thinking

highly either of men or of matrimony, marriage had always been her object; it was the only honourable provision for well-educated young women of small fortune, and however uncertain of giving happiness, must be their pleasantest preservative from want. This preservative she had now obtained; and at the age of twenty-seven, without having ever been handsome, she felt all the good luck of it. The least agreeable circumstance in the business was the surprise it must occasion to Elizabeth Bennet, whose friendship she valued beyond that of any other person. Elizabeth would wonder, and probably would blame her; and though her resolution was not to be shaken, her feelings must be hurt by such a disapprobation. She resolved to give her the information herself, and therefore charged Mr. Collins, when he returned to Longbourn to dinner, to drop no hint of what had passed before any of the family. A promise of secrecy was of course very dutifully given, but it could not be kept without difficulty; for the curiosity excited by his long absence burst forth in such very direct questions on his return as required some ingenuity to evade, and he was at the same time exercising great self-denial, for he was longing to publish his prosperous love.

As he was to begin his journey too early on the

morrow to see any of the family, the ceremony of leavetaking was performed when the ladies moved for the night; and Mrs. Bennet, with great politeness and cordiality, said how happy they should be to see him at Longbourn again, whenever his other engagements might allow him to visit them.

'My dear madam,' he replied, 'this invitation is particularly gratifying, because it is what I have been hoping to receive; and you may be very certain that I shall avail myself of it as soon as possible.'

They were all astonished; and Mr. Bennet, who could by no means wish for so speedy a return, immediately said—

'But is there not danger of Lady Catherine's disapprobation here, my good sir? You had better neglect your relations than run the risk of offending your patroness.'

'My dear sir,' replied Mr. Collins, 'I am particularly obliged to you for this friendly caution, and you may depend upon my not taking so material a step without her ladyship's concurrence.'

'You cannot be too much on your guard. Risk anything rather than her displeasure; and if you find it likely to be raised by your coming to us again, which I should think exceedingly probable, stay quietly at home, and be satisfied that *we* shall take no offence.'

'Believe me, my dear sir, my gratitude is warmly excited by such affectionate attention; and depend upon it, you will speedily receive from me a letter of thanks for this, as for every other mark of your regard during my stay in Hertfordshire. As for my fair cousins, though my absence may not be long enough to render it necessary, I shall now take the liberty of wishing them health and happiness, not excepting my cousin Elizabeth.'

With proper civilities the ladies then withdrew; all of them equally surprised to find that he meditated a quick return. Mrs. Bennet wished to understand by it that he thought of paying his addresses to one of her younger girls, and Mary might have been prevailed on to accept him. She rated his abilities much higher than any of the others; there was a solidity in his reflections which often struck her, and though by no 'means so clever as herself, she thought that if encouraged to read and improve himself by such an example as hers, he might become a very agreeable companion. But on the following morning every hope of this kind was done away. Miss Lucas called soon after breakfast, and in a private conference with Elizabeth related the event of the day before.

The possibility of Mr. Collins's fancying himself in love with her friend had once occurred

to Elizabeth within the last day or two; but
that Charlotte could encourage him seemed
almost as far from possibility as that she could
encourage him herself, and her astonishment
was consequently so great as to overcome at
first the bounds of decorum, and she could not
help crying out—

'Engaged to Mr. Collins! my dear Charlotte,
impossible!'

The steady countenance which Miss Lucas
had commanded in telling her story, gave way
to a momentary confusion here on receiving
so direct a reproach; though, as it was no
more than she expected, she soon regained her
composure, and calmly replied—

'Why should you be surprised, my dear Eliza?
Do you think it incredible that Mr. Collins
should be able to procure any woman's good
opinion, because he was not so happy as to
succeed with you?'

But Elizabeth had now recollected herself,
and making a strong effort for it, was able to
assure her with tolerable firmness that the prospect of their relationship was highly grateful
to her, and that she wished her all imaginable
happiness.

'I see what you are feeling,' replied Charlotte;
'you must be surprised, very much surprised—
so lately as Mr. Collins was wishing to marry

you. But when you have had time to think it all over, I hope you will be satisfied with what I have done. I am not romantic, you know; I never was. I ask only a comfortable home; and considering Mr. Collins's character, connexions, and situation in life, I am convinced that my chance of happiness with him is as fair as most people can boast on entering the marriage state.'

Elizabeth quietly answered 'Undoubtedly'; and after an awkward pause they returned to the rest of the family. Charlotte did not stay much longer, and Elizabeth was then left to reflect on what she had heard. It was a long time before she became at all reconciled to the idea of so unsuitable a match. The strangeness of Mr. Collins's making two offers of marriage within three days was nothing in comparison of his being now accepted. She had always felt that Charlotte's opinion of matrimony was not exactly like her own, but she could not have supposed it possible that, when called into action, she would have sacrificed every better feeling to worldly advantage. Charlotte the wife of Mr. Collins was a most humiliating picture! And to the pang of a friend disgracing herself and sunk in her esteem, was added the distressing conviction that it was impossible for that friend to be tolerably happy in the lot she had chosen.

CHAPTER XXIII

ELIZABETH was sitting with her mother and sisters, reflecting on what she had heard, and doubting whether she was authorised to mention it, when Sir William Lucas himself appeared, sent by his daughter to announce her engagement to the family. With many compliments to them, and much self-gratulation on the prospect of a connexion between the houses, he unfolded the matter—to an audience not merely wondering, but incredulous; for Mrs. Bennet, with more perseverance than politeness, protested he must be entirely mistaken; and Lydia, always unguarded and often uncivil, boisterously exclaimed—

'Good Lord! Sir William, how can you tell such a story? Do not you know that Mr. Collins wants to marry Lizzy?'

Nothing less than the complaisance of a courtier could have borne without anger such treatment; but Sir William's good-breeding carried him through it all; and though he begged leave to be positive as to the truth of his information, he listened to all their impertinence with the most forbearing courtesy.

Elizabeth, feeling it incumbent on her to relieve him from so unpleasant a situation, now put herself ·forward to confirm his account, by mentioning her prior knowledge of it from Charlotte herself; and endeavoured to put a stop to the exclamations of her mother and sisters by the earnestness of her congratulations to Sir William, in which she was readily joined by Jane, and by making a variety of remarks on the happiness that might be expected from the match, the excellent character of Mr. Collins, and the convenient distance of Hunsford from London.

Mrs. Bennet was, in fact, too much overpowered to say a great deal while Sir William remained; but no sooner had he left them than her feelings found a rapid vent. In the first place, she persisted in disbelieving the whole of the matter; secondly, she was very sure that Mr. Collins had been taken in; thirdly, she trusted that they would never be happy together; and fourthly, that the match might be broken off. Two inferences, however, were plainly deduced from the whole: one, that Elizabeth was the real cause of all the mischief; and the other, that she herself had been barbarously used by them all; and on these two . points she principally dwelt during the rest of the day.

Nothing could console and nothing appease her. Nor did that day wear out her resentment. A week elapsed before she could see Elizabeth without scolding her, a month passed away before she could speak to Sir William or Lady Lucas without being rude, and many months were gone before she could at all forgive their daughter.

Mr. Bennet's emotions were much more tranquil on the occasion, and such as he did experience he pronounced to be of a most agreeable sort; for it gratified him, he said, to discover that Charlotte Lucas, whom he had been used to think tolerably sensible, was as foolish as his wife, and more foolish than his daughter!

Jane confessed herself a little surprised at the match; but she said less of her astonishment than of her earnest desire for their happiness; nor could Elizabeth persuade her to consider it as improbable. Kitty and Lydia were far from envying Miss Lucas, for Mr. Collins was only a clergyman; and it affected them in no other way than as a piece of news to spread at Meryton.

Lady Lucas could not be insensible of triumph on being able to retort on Mrs. Bennet the comfort of having a daughter well married; and she called at Longbourn rather oftener than usual to say how happy she was, though Mrs. Bennet's sour looks and ill-natured remarks might have been enough to drive happiness away.

Between Elizabeth and Charlotte there was a restraint which kept them mutually silent on the subject; and Elizabeth felt persuaded that no real confidence could ever subsist between them again. Her disappointment in Charlotte made her turn with fonder regard to her sister, of whose rectitude and delicacy she was sure her opinion could never be shaken, and for whose happiness she grew daily more anxious, as Bingley had now been gone a week, and nothing was heard of his return.

Jane had sent Caroline an early answer to her letter, and was counting the days till she might reasonably hope to hear again. The promised letter of thanks from Mr. Collins arrived on Tuesday, addressed to their father, and written with all the solemnity of gratitude which a twelvemonth's abode in the family might have prompted. After discharging his conscience on that head, he proceeded to inform them, with many rapturous expressions, of his happiness in having obtained the affection of their amiable neighbour, Miss Lucas, and then explained that it was merely with the view of enjoying her society that he had been so ready to close with their kind wish of seeing him again at Long-bourn, whither he hoped to be able to return on

Monday fortnight; for Lady Catherine, he added, so heartily approved his marriage that she wished it to take place as soon as possible, which he trusted would be an unanswerable argument with his amiable Charlotte to name an early day for making him the happiest of men.

Mr. Collins's return into Hertfordshire was no longer a matter of pleasure to Mrs. Bennet. On the contrary, she was as much disposed to complain of it as her husband.—It was very strange that he should come to Longbourn instead of to Lucas Lodge; it was also very inconvenient and exceedingly troublesome.—She hated having visitors in the house while her health was so indifferent, and lovers were of all people the most disagreeable. Such were the gentle murmurs of Mrs. Bennet, and they gave way only to the greater distress of Mr. Bingley's continued absence.

Neither Jane nor Elizabeth were comfortable on this subject. Day after day passed away without bringing any other tidings of him than the report which shortly prevailed in Meryton of his coming no more to Netherfield the whole winter; a report which highly incensed Mrs. Bennet, and which she never failed to contradict as a most scandalous falsehood.

Even Elizabeth began to fear — not that Bingley was indifferent—but that his sisters

3 N*   197

would be successful in keeping him away. Unwilling as she was to admit an idea so destructive of Jane's happiness, and so dishonourable to the stability of her lover, she could not prevent its frequently recurring. The united efforts of his two unfeeling sisters and of his overpowering friend, assisted by the attractions of Miss Darcy and the amusements of London, might be too much, she feared, for the strength of his attachment.

As for Jane, *her* anxiety under this suspense was, of course, more painful than Elizabeth's; but whatever she felt she was desirous of concealing, and between herself and Elizabeth, therefore, the subject was never alluded to. But as no such delicacy restrained her mother, an hour seldom passed in which she did not talk of Bingley, express her impatience for his arrival, or even require Jane to confess that if he did not come back, she should think herself very ill used. It needed all Jane's steady mildness to bear these attacks with tolerable tranquillity.

Mr. Collins returned most punctually on the Monday fortnight, but his reception at Longbourn was not quite so gracious as it had been on his first introduction. He was too happy, however, to need much attention; and, luckily for the others, the business of love-making relieved them from a great deal of his company.

198

The chief of every day was spent by him at Lucas Lodge, and he sometimes returned to Longbourn only in time to make an apology for his absence before the family went to bed.

Mrs. Bennet was really in a most pitiable state. The very mention of anything concerning the match threw her into an agony of ill-humour, and wherever she went she was sure of hearing it talked of. The sight of Miss Lucas was odious to her. As her successor in that house, she regarded her with jealous abhorrence. Whenever Charlotte came to see them, she concluded her to be anticipating the hour of possession; and whenever she spoke in a low voice to Mr. Collins, was convinced that they were talking of the Longbourn estate, and resolving to turn herself and her daughters out of the house as soon as Mr. Bennet were dead. She complained bitterly of all this to her husband.

'Indeed, Mr. Bennet,' said she, 'it is very hard to think that Charlotte Lucas should ever be mistress of this house, that *I* should be forced to make way for *her*, and live to see her take my place in it!'

'My dear, do not give way to such gloomy thoughts. Let us hope for better things. Let us flatter ourselves that *I* may be the survivor.'

This was not very consoling to Mrs. Bennet,

and therefore, instead of making any answer, she went on as before.

'I cannot bear to think that they should have all this estate. If it was not for the entail, I should not mind it.'

'What should not you mind?'

'I should not mind anything at all.'

'Let us be thankful that you are preserved from a state of such insensibility.'

'I never can be thankful, Mr. Bennet, for anything about the entail. How any one could have the conscience to entail away an estate from one's own daughters, I cannot understand; and all for the sake of Mr. Collins too!—Why should *he* have it more than anybody else?'

'I leave it to yourself to determine,' said Mr. Bennet.

CHAPTER XXIV

Miss Bingley's letter arrived, and put an end to doubt. The very first sentence conveyed the assurance of their being all settled in London for the winter, and concluded with her brother's regret at not having had time to pay his respects to his friends in Hertfordshire before he left the country.

Hope was over, entirely over; and when Jane could attend to the rest of the letter, she found little, except the professed affection of the writer, that could give her any comfort. Miss Darcy's praise occupied the chief of it. Her many attractions were again dwelt on, and Caroline boasted joyfully of their increasing intimacy, and ventured to predict the accomplishment of the wishes which had been unfolded in her former letter. She wrote also with great pleasure of her brother's being an inmate of Mr. Darcy's house, and mentioned with raptures some plans of the latter with regard to new furniture.

Elizabeth, to whom Jane very soon communi-

201

cated the chief of all this, heard it in silent
indignation. Her heart was divided between
concern for her sister and resentment against all
others. To Caroline's assertion of her brother's
being partial to Miss Darcy she paid no credit.
That he was really fond of Jane, she doubted
no more than she had ever done; and much as
she had always been disposed to like him, she
could not think without anger, hardly without
contempt, on that easiness of temper, that want
of proper resolution, which now made him the
slave of his designing friends, and led him to
sacrifice his own happiness to the caprice of
their inclinations. Had his own happiness, however, been the only sacrifice, he might have been
allowed to sport with it in whatever manner he
thought best; but her sister's was involved in
it, as she thought he must be sensible himself.
It was a subject, in short, on which reflection
would be long indulged, and must be unavail-
ing. She could think of nothing else; and yet
whether Bingley's regard had really died away,
or were suppressed by his friends' interference;
whether he had been aware of Jane's attachment, or whether it had escaped his observation;
whatever were the case, though her opinion of
him must be materially affected by the difference, her sister's situation remained the same,
her peace equally wounded.

A day or two passed before Jane had courage to speak of her feelings to Elizabeth ; but at last, on Mrs. Bennet's leaving them together, after a longer irritation than usual about Netherfield and its master, she could not help saying—

'O that my dear mother had more command over herself! she can have no idea of the pain she gives me by her continual reflections on him. But I will not repine. It cannot last long. He will be forgot, and we shall all be as we were before.'

Elizabeth looked at her sister with incredulous solicitude, but said nothing.

'You doubt me,' cried Jane, slightly colouring ; 'indeed you have no reason. He may live in my memory as the most amiable man of my acquaintance, but that is all. I have nothing either to hope or fear, and nothing to reproach him with. Thank God! I have not *that* pain. A little time therefore,— I shall certainly try to get the better.'

With a stronger voice she soon added, 'I have this comfort immediately, that it has not been more than an error of fancy on my side, and that it has done no harm to any one but myself.'

'My dear Jane!' exclaimed Elizabeth, 'you are too good. Your sweetness and disinterestedness are really angelic ; I do not know what to say to you. I feel as if I had never done you justice, or loved you as you deserve.'

Miss Bennet eagerly disclaimed all extraordinary merit, and threw back the praise on her sister's warm affection.

'Nay,' said Elizabeth, 'this is not fair. *You* wish to think all the world respectable, and are hurt if I speak ill of anybody. *I* only want to think *you* perfect, and you set yourself against it. Do not be afraid of my running into any excess, of my encroaching on your privilege of universal goodwill. You need not. There are few people whom I really love, and still fewer of whom I think well. The more I see of the world, the more am I dissatisfied with it; and every day confirms my belief of the inconsistency of all human characters, and of the little dependence that can be placed on the appearance of either merit or sense. I have met with two instances lately: one I will not mention, the other is Charlotte's marriage. It is unaccountable! in every view it is unaccountable!'

'My dear Lizzy, do not give way to such feelings as these. They will ruin your happiness. You do not make allowance enough for difference of situation and temper. Consider Mr. Collins's respectability, and Charlotte's prudent, steady character. Remember that she is one of a large family; that as to fortune it is a most eligible match; and be ready to believe, for everybody's sake, that she may feel something like regard and esteem for our cousin.'

'To oblige you, I would try to believe almost anything, but no one else could be benefited by such a belief as this; for were I persuaded that Charlotte had any regard for him, I should only think worse of her understanding than I now do of her heart. My dear Jane, Mr. Collins is a conceited, pompous, narrow-minded, silly man : you know he is, as well as I do; and you must feel, as well as I do, that the woman who marries him cannot have a proper way of thinking. You shall not defend her, though it is Charlotte Lucas. You shall not, for the sake of one individual, change the meaning of principle and integrity, nor endeavour to persuade yourself or me that selfishness is prudence, and insensibility of danger security for happiness.'

'I must think your language too strong in speaking of both,' replied Jane; 'and I hope you will be convinced of it by seeing them happy together. But enough of this. You alluded to something else. You mentioned *two* instances. I cannot misunderstand you, but I entreat you, dear Lizzy, not to pain me by thinking *that person* to blame, and saying your opinion of him is sunk. We must not be so ready to fancy ourselves intentionally injured. We must not expect a lively young man to be always so guarded and circumspect. It is very often nothing but our own vanity that deceives us. Women fancy admiration means more than it does.'

'And men take care that they should.'

'If it is designedly done, they cannot be justified; but I have no idea of there being so much design in the world as some persons imagine.'

'I am far from attributing any part of Mr. Bingley's conduct to design,' said Elizabeth; 'but without scheming to do wrong, or to make others unhappy, there may be error, and there may be misery. Thoughtlessness, want of attention to other people's feelings, and want of resolution, will do the business.'

'And do you impute it to either of those?'

'Yes; to the last. But if I go on, I shall displease you by saying what I think of persons you esteem. Stop me whilst you can.'

'You persist, then, in supposing his sisters influence him?'

'Yes, in conjunction with his friend.'

'I cannot believe it. Why should they try to influence him? They can only wish his happiness; and if he is attached to me, no other woman can secure it.'

'Your first position is false. They may wish

many things besides his happiness ; they may wish
his increase of wealth and consequence ; they may
wish him to marry a girl who has all the importance of money, great connexions, and pride.'

'Beyond a doubt they do wish him to chuse
Miss Darcy,' replied Jane ; 'but this may be
from better feelings than you are supposing.
They have known her much longer than they
have known me : no wonder if they love her
better.   But, whatever may be their own wishes,
it is very unlikely they should have opposed
their brother's.   What sister would think herself
at liberty to do it, unless there were something very objectionable ?   If they believed him
attached to me, they would not try to part us ;
if he were so, they could not succeed.   By supposing such an affection, you make everybody
acting unnaturally and wrong, and me most
unhappy.   Do not distress me by the idea.   I
am not ashamed of having been mistaken—or,
at least, it is slight, it is nothing in comparison
of what I should feel in thinking ill of him or
his sisters.   Let me take it in the best light, in
the light in which it may be understood.'

Elizabeth could not oppose such a wish ; and
from this time Mr. Bingley's name was scarcely
ever mentioned between them.

Mrs. Bennet still continued to wonder and
repine at his returning no more, and though a

day seldom passed in which Elizabeth did not
account for it clearly, there seemed little chance
of her ever considering it with less perplexity.
Her daughter endeavoured to convince her of
what she did not believe herself, that his attentions to Jane had been merely the effect of a
common and transient liking, which ceased when
he saw her no more; but though the probability
of the statement was admitted at the time, she
had the same story to repeat every day. Mrs.
Bennet's best comfort was that Mr. Bingley
must be down again in the summer.

Mr. Bennet treated the matter differently.
'So, Lizzy,' said he one day, 'your sister is
crossed in love, I find. I congratulate her.
Next to being married, a girl likes to be crossed
in love a little now and then. It is something
to think of, and gives her a sort of distinction
among her companions. When is your turn to
come? You will hardly bear to be long out-
done by Jane. Now is your time. Here are
officers enough at Meryton to disappoint all the
young ladies in the country. Let Wickham be
your man. He is a pleasant fellow, and would
jilt you creditably.'

'Thank you, sir, but a less agreeable man
would satisfy me. We must not all expect
Jane's good fortune.'

'True,' said Mr. Bennet, 'but it is a comfort
208

to think that whatever of that kind may befall you, you have an affectionate mother who will always make the most of it.'

Mr. Wickham's society was of material service in dispelling the gloom which the late perverse occurrences had thrown on many of the Longbourn family. They saw him often, and to his other recommendations was now added that of general unreserve. The whole of what Elizabeth had already heard, his claims on Mr. Darcy, and all that he had suffered from him, was now openly acknowledged and publicly canvassed; and everybody was pleased to think how much they had always disliked Mr. Darcy before they had known anything of the matter.

Miss Bennet was the only creature who could suppose there might be any extenuating circumstances in the case, unknown to the society of Hertfordshire; her mild and steady candour always pleaded for allowances, and urged the possibility of mistakes—but by everybody else Mr. Darcy was condemned as the worst of men.

CHAPTER XXV

AFTER a week spent in professions of love and schemes of felicity, Mr. Collins was called from his amiable Charlotte by the arrival of Saturday. The pain of separation, however, might be alleviated on his side, by preparations for the reception of his bride; as he had reason to hope that, shortly after his next return into Hertfordshire, the day would be fixed that was to make him the happiest of men. He took leave of his relations at Longbourn with as much solemnity as before; wished his fair cousins health and happiness again, and promised their father another letter of thanks.

On the following Monday Mrs. Bennet had the pleasure of receiving her brother and his wife, who came as usual to spend the Christmas at Longbourn. Mr. Gardiner was a sensible, gentlemanlike man, greatly superior to his sister, as well by nature as education. The Netherfield ladies would have had difficulty in believing that a man who lived by trade, and within view of his own warehouses, could have been so well-bred and agreeable. Mrs. Gardiner, who was several years younger than Mrs. Bennet and Mrs. Philips, was an amiable, intelligent, elegant woman, and a great favourite with all her Longbourn nieces. Between the two eldest and herself especially there subsisted a very particular regard. They had frequently been staying with her in town.

The first part of Mrs. Gardiner's business on her arrival was to distribute her presents and describe the newest fashions. When this was done she had a less active part to play. It became her turn to listen. Mrs. Bennet had many grievances to relate, and much to complain of. They had all been very ill-used since she last saw her sister. Two of her girls had been on the point of marriage, and after all there was nothing in it.

'I do not blame Jane,' she continued, 'for Jane would have got Mr. Bingley if she could. But Lizzy! oh, sister! it is very hard to think that she might have been Mr. Collins's wife by this time, had not it been for her own perverseness. He made her an offer in this very room, and she refused him. The consequence of it is, that Lady Lucas will have a daughter married before I have, and that Longbourn estate is just as much entailed as ever. The Lucases are very artful people indeed, sister. They are all for what they can get. I am sorry to say it of them, but so it is. It makes me very nervous and poorly to be thwarted so in my own family, and to have neighbours who think of themselves before anybody else. However, your coming just at this time is the greatest of comforts, and I am very glad to hear what you tell us of long sleeves.'

Mrs. Gardiner, to whom the chief of this news had been given before, in the course of Jane and Elizabeth's correspondence with her, made her sister a slight answer, and, in compassion to her nieces, turned the conversation.

When alone with Elizabeth afterwards, she spoke more on the subject. 'It seems likely to have been a desirable match for Jane,' said she. 'I am sorry it went off. But these things happen so often! A young man, such as you describe Mr. Bingley, so easily falls in love with a pretty girl for a few weeks, and when accident separates them, so easily forgets her, that these sort of inconstancies are very frequent.'

'An excellent consolation in its way,' said Elizabeth, 'but it will not do for *us*. We do not suffer by accident. It does not often happen that the interference of friends will persuade a young man of independent fortune to think no more of a girl whom he was violently in love with only a few days before.'

'But that expression of "violently in love"
212

is so hackneyed, so doubtful, so indefinite, that it gives me very little idea. It is as often applied to feelings which arise from an half-hour's acquaintance, as to a real, strong attachment. Pray, how *violent was* Mr. Bingley's love?'

'I never saw a more promising inclination; he was growing quite inattentive to other people, and wholly engrossed by her. Every time they met it was more decided and remarkable. At his own ball he offended two or three young ladies by not asking them to dance; and I spoke to him twice myself without receiving an answer. Could there be finer symptoms? Is not general incivility the very essence of love?'

'Oh yes!—of that kind of love which I suppose him to have felt. Poor Jane! I am sorry for her, because, with her disposition, she may not get over it immediately. It had better have happened to *you*, Lizzy; you would have laughed yourself out of it sooner. But do you think she would be prevailed on to go back with us? Change of scene might be of service—and perhaps a little relief from home may be as useful as anything.'

Elizabeth was exceedingly pleased with this proposal, and felt persuaded of her sister's ready acquiescence.

'I hope,' added Mrs. Gardiner, 'that no con-

3 o*

sideration with regard to this young man will
influence her. We live in so different a part
of town, all our connexions are so different,
and, as you well know, we go out so little, that
it is very improbable that they should meet at
all, unless he really comes to see her.'

'And *that* is quite impossible; for he is now
in the custody of his friend, and Mr. Darcy would
no more suffer him to call on Jane in such a
part of London! My dear aunt, how could you
think of it? Mr. Darcy may, perhaps, have
heard of such a place as Gracechurch Street,
but he would hardly think a month's ablution
enough to cleanse him from its impurities, were
he once to enter it; and, depend upon it, Mr.
Bingley never stirs without him.'

'So much the better. I hope they will not
meet at all. But does not Jane correspond
with his sister? *She* will not be able to help
calling.'

'She will drop the acquaintance entirely.'

But in spite of the certainty in which Elizabeth affected to place this point, as well as the
still more interesting one of Bingley's being
withheld from seeing Jane, she felt a solicitude
on the subject which convinced her, on examination, that she did not consider it entirely hopeless. It was possible, and sometimes she thought
it probable, that his affection might be reuni-

mated, and the influence of his friends successfully combated by the more natural influence of Jane's attractions.

Miss Bennet accepted her aunt's invitation with pleasure; and the Bingleys were no otherwise in her thoughts at the same time than as she hoped, by Caroline's not living in the same house with her brother, she might occasionally spend a morning with her, without any danger of seeing him.

The Gardiners staid a week at Longbourn; and what with the Philipses, the Lucases, and the officers, there was not a day without its engagement. Mrs. Bennet had so carefully provided for the entertainment of her brother and sister that they did not once sit down to a family dinner. When the engagement was for home, some of the officers always made part of it—of which officers Mr. Wickham was sure to be one; and on these occasions Mrs. Gardiner, rendered suspicious by Elizabeth's warm commendation of him, narrowly observed them both. Without supposing them, from what she saw, to be very seriously in love, their preference of each other was plain enough to make her a little uneasy; and she resolved to speak to Elizabeth on the subject before she left Hertfordshire, and represent to her the imprudence of encouraging such an attachment.

To Mrs. Gardiner, Wickham had one means of affording pleasure, unconnected with his general powers. About ten or a dozen years ago, before her marriage, she had spent a considerable time in that very part of Derbyshire to which he belonged. They had, therefore, many acquaintance in common; and though Wickham had been little there since the death of Darcy's father, five years before, it was yet in his power to give her fresher intelligence of her former friends than she had been in the way of procuring.

Mrs. Gardiner had seen Pemberley, and known the late Mr. Darcy by character perfectly well. Here consequently was an inexhaustible subject of discourse. In comparing her recollection of Pemberley with the minute description which Wickham could give, and in bestowing her tribute of praise on the character of its late possessor, she was delighting both him and herself. On being made acquainted with the present Mr. Darcy's treatment of him, she tried to remember something of that gentleman's reputed disposition when quite a lad which might agree with it, and was confident at last that she recollected having heard Mr. Fitzwilliam Darcy formerly spoken of as a very proud, ill-natured boy.

216

CHAPTER XXVI

Mrs. Gardiner's caution to Elizabeth was punctually and kindly given on the first favourable opportunity of speaking to her alone: after honestly telling her what she thought, she thus went on—

'You are too sensible a girl, Lizzy, to fall in love merely because you are warned against it; and therefore I am not afraid of speaking openly. Seriously, I would have you be on your guard. Do not involve yourself or endeavour to involve him in an affection which the want of fortune would make so very imprudent. I have nothing to say against *him*: he is a most interesting young man; and if he had the fortune he ought to have, I should think you could not do better. But as it is, you must not let your fancy run away with you. You have sense, and we all expect you to use it. Your father would depend on *your* resolution and good conduct, I am sure. You must not disappoint your father.'

'My dear aunt, this is being serious indeed.'

217

'Yes, and I hope to engage you to be serious likewise.'

'Well, then, you need not be under any alarm. I will take care of myself, and of Mr. Wickham too. He shall not be in love with me, if I can prevent it.'

'Elizabeth, you are not serious now.'

'I beg your pardon, I will try again. At present I am not in love with Mr. Wickham; no, I certainly am not. But he is, beyond all comparison, the most agreeable man I ever saw —and if he becomes really attached to me— I believe it will be better that he should not. I see the imprudence of it.—Oh! *that* abominable Mr. Darcy!—My father's opinion of me does me the greatest honour, and I should be miserable to forfeit it. My father, however, is partial to Mr. Wickham. In short, my dear aunt, I should be very sorry to be the means of making any of you unhappy; but since we see every day that where there is affection, young people are seldom withheld by immediate want of fortune from entering into engagements with each other, how can I promise to be wiser than so many of my fellow-creatures if I am tempted, or how am I even to know that it would be wisdom to resist? All that I can promise you, therefore, is not to be in a hurry. I will not be in a hurry to believe myself his first object. When I am in company with him, I will not be wishing. In short, I will do my best.'

'Perhaps it will be as well if you discourage his coming here so very often. At least you should not *remind* your mother of inviting him.'

'As I did the other day,' said Elizabeth, with a conscious smile; 'very true, it will be wise in me to refrain from *that*. But do not imagine that he is always here so often. It is on your account that he has been so frequently invited this week. You know my mother's ideas as to the necessity of constant company for her friends. But really, and upon my honour, I will try to do what I think to be the wisest; and now I hope you are satisfied.'

Her aunt assured her that she was, and Elizabeth having thanked her for the kindness of her hints, they parted;—a wonderful instance of advice being given on such a point without being resented.

Mr. Collins returned into Hertfordshire soon after it had been quitted by the Gardiners and Jane; but as he took up his abode with the Lucases, his arrival was no great inconvenience to Mrs. Bennet. His marriage was now fast approaching, and she was at length so far resigned as to think it inevitable, and even repeatedly to say, in an ill-natured tone, that she '*wished* they might be happy.' Thursday was to be the wedding day, and on Wednesday Miss Lucas paid her farewell visit; and when she rose to take leave, Elizabeth, ashamed of her mother's ungracious and reluctant good wishes, and sincerely affected herself, accompanied her out of the room. As they went downstairs together Charlotte said—

'I shall depend on hearing from you very often, Eliza.'

'*That* you certainly shall.'

'And I have another favour to ask. Will you come and see me?'

'We shall often meet, I hope, in Hertfordshire.'

'I am not likely to leave Kent for some time. Promise me, therefore, to come to Hunsford.'

Elizabeth could not refuse, though she foresaw little pleasure in the visit.

'My father and Maria are to come to me in March,' added Charlotte, 'and I hope you will consent to be of the party. Indeed, Eliza, you will be as welcome to me as either of them.'

The wedding took place: the bride and bridegroom set off for Kent from the church door, and everybody had as much to say, or to hear, on the subject as usual. Elizabeth soon heard from her friend; and their correspondence was as regular and frequent as it had ever been; that it should be equally unreserved was impossible.

Elizabeth could never address her without feeling
that all the comfort of intimacy was over; and
though determined not to slacken as a corre-
spondent, it was for the sake of what had been
rather than what was. Charlotte's first letters
were received with a good deal of eagerness;
there could not but be curiosity to know how
she would speak of her new home, how she
would like Lady Catherine, and how happy she
would dare pronounce herself to be; though,
when the letters were read, Elizabeth felt that
Charlotte expressed herself on every point exactly
as she might have foreseen. She wrote cheer-
fully, seemed surrounded with comforts, and
mentioned nothing which she could not praise.
The house, furniture, neighbourhood, and roads
were all to her taste, and Lady Catherine's behaviour was most friendly and obliging. It was
Mr. Collins's picture of Hunsford and Rosings
rationally softened; and Elizabeth perceived
that she must wait for her own visit there to
know the rest.

Jane had already written a few lines to her
sister to announce their safe arrival in London;
and when she wrote again, Elizabeth hoped it
would be in her power to say something of the
Bingleys.

Her impatience for this second letter was as
well rewarded as impatience generally is. Jane

had been a week in town without either seeing
or hearing from Caroline.   She accounted for it,
however, by supposing that her last letter to her
friend from Longbourn had, by some accident,
been lost.

'My aunt,' she continued, 'is going to-morrow
into that part of the town, and I shall take the
opportunity of calling in Grosvenor Street.'

She wrote again when the visit was paid, and
she had seen Miss Bingley. 'I did not think
Caroline in spirits,' were her words; 'but she was
very glad to see me, and reproached me for
giving her no notice of my coming to London.
I was right, therefore; my last letter had never
reached her. I inquired after their brother, of
course. He was well, but so much engaged
with Mr. Darcy that they scarcely ever saw him.
I found that Miss Darcy was expected to dinner.
I wish I could see her. My visit was not long,
as Caroline and Mrs. Hurst were going out. I
dare say I shall soon see them here.'

Elizabeth shook her head over this letter. It
convinced her that accident only could discover
to Mr. Bingley her sister's being in town.

Four weeks passed away, and Jane saw nothing of him. She endeavoured to persuade
herself that she did not regret it; but she could
no longer be blind to Miss Bingley's inattention.
After waiting at home every morning for a

fortnight, and inventing every evening a fresh excuse for her, the visitor did at last appear; but the shortness of her stay, and yet more, the alteration of her manner, would allow Jane to deceive herself no longer. The letter which she wrote on this occasion to her sister will prove what she felt.

'My dearest Lizzy will, I am sure, be incapable of triumphing in her better judgment, at my expense, when I confess myself to have been entirely deceived in Miss Bingley's regard for me. But, my dear sister, though the event has proved you right, do not think me obstinate if I still assert that, considering what her behaviour was, my confidence was as natural as your suspicion. I do not at all comprehend her reason for wishing to be intimate with me; but if the same circumstances were to happen again, I am sure I should be deceived again. Caroline did not return my visit till yesterday; and not a note, not a line, did I receive in the meantime. When she did come, it was very evident that she had no pleasure in it; she made a slight, formal apology for not calling before, said not a word of wishing to see me again, and was in every respect so altered a creature, that when she went away I was perfectly resolved to continue the acquaintance no longer. I pity, though

I cannot help blaming her. She was very wrong
in singling me out as she did; I can safely say
that every advance to intimacy began on her
side. But I pity her, because she must feel
that she has been acting wrong, and because I
am very sure that anxiety for her brother is the
cause of it. I need not explain myself farther;
and though *we* know this anxiety to be quite
needless, yet if she feels it, it will easily account
for her behaviour to me; and so deservedly dear
as he is to his sister, whatever anxiety she may
feel on his behalf is natural and amiable. I cannot but wonder, however, at her having any such
fears now, because, if he had at all cared about
me, we must have met long, long ago. He
knows of my being in town, I am certain, from
something she said herself; and yet it would
seem, by her manner of talking, as if she wanted
to persuade herself that he is really partial to
Miss Darcy. I cannot understand it. If I
were not afraid of judging harshly, I should be
almost tempted to say that there is a strong
appearance of duplicity in all this. But I will
endeavour to banish every painful thought, and
think only of what will make me happy—your
affection, and the invariable kindness of my dear
uncle and aunt. Let me hear from you very
soon. Miss Bingley said something of his never
returning to Netherfield again, of giving up the

house, but not with any certainty. We had better not mention it. I am extremely glad that you have such pleasant accounts from our friends at Hunsford. Pray go to see them, with Sir William and Maria. I am sure you will be very comfortable there.—Yours, etc.'

This letter gave Elizabeth some pain; but her spirits returned as she considered that Jane would no longer be duped by the sister at least. All expectation from the brother was now absolutely over. She would not even wish for any renewal of his attentions. His character sunk on every review of it ; and as a punishment for him, as well as a possible advantage to Jane, she seriously hoped he might really soon marry Mr. Darcy's sister, as by Wickham's account, she would make him abundantly regret what he had thrown away.

Mrs. Gardiner about this time reminded Elizabeth of her promise concerning that gentleman, and required information ; and Elizabeth had such to send as might rather give contentment to her aunt than to herself. His apparent partiality had subsided, his attentions were over, he was the admirer of some one else. Elizabeth was watchful enough to see it all, but she could see it and write of it without material pain. Her heart had been but slightly touched, and her vanity was satisfied with believing that *she* would have been his only choice, had fortune permitted it. The sudden acquisition of ten thousand pounds was the most remarkable charm of the young lady to whom he was now rendering himself agreeable; but Elizabeth, less clear-sighted perhaps in this case than in Charlotte's, did not quarrel with him for his wish of independence. Nothing, on the contrary, could be more natural; and while able to suppose that it cost him a few struggles to relinquish her, she was ready to allow it a wise and desirable measure for both, and could very sincerely wish him happy.

All this was acknowledged to Mrs. Gardiner; and after relating the circumstances, she thus went on :—' I am now convinced, my dear aunt, that I have never been much in love; for had I really experienced that pure and elevating passion, I should at present detest his very name, and wish him all manner of evil. But my feelings are not only cordial towards *him*; they are even impartial towards Miss King. I cannot find out that I hate her at all, or that I am in the least unwilling to think her a very good sort of girl. There can be no love in all this. My watchfulness has been effectual; and though I should certainly be a more interesting object to all my acquaintance were I distractedly in love with him, I cannot say that I regret my comparative insignificance. Importance may sometimes be purchased too dearly. Kitty and Lydia take his defection much more to heart than I do. They are young in the ways of the world, and not yet open to the mortifying conviction that handsome young men must have something to live on as well as the plain.'

CHAPTER XXVII

With no greater events than these in the Longbourn family, and otherwise diversified by little
beyond the walks to Meryton, sometimes dirty
and sometimes cold, did January and February
pass away.   March was to take Elizabeth to
Hunsford.   She had not at first thought very
seriously of going thither; but Charlotte, she
soon found, was depending on the plan, and
she gradually learnt to consider it herself with
greater pleasure as well as greater certainty.
Absence had increased her desire of seeing
Charlotte again, and weakened her disgust of
Mr. Collins.   There was novelty in the scheme,
and as, with such a mother and such uncom-
panionable sisters, home could not be faultless,
a little change was not unwelcome for its own
sake.   The journey would, moreover, give her a
peep at Jane; and, in short, as the time drew
near, she would have been very sorry for any
delay.   Everything, however, went on smoothly,
and was finally settled according to Charlotte's
first sketch.   She was to accompany Sir William

and his second daughter. The improvement of spending a night in London was added in time, and the plan became perfect as plan could be.

The only pain was in leaving her father, who would certainly miss her, and who, when it came to the point, so little liked her going, that he told her to write to him, and almost promised to answer her letter.

The farewell between herself and Mr. Wickham was perfectly friendly; on his side even more. His present pursuit could not make him forget that Elizabeth had been the first to excite and to deserve his attention, the first to listen and to pity, the first to be admired; and in his manner of bidding her adieu, wishing her every enjoyment, reminding her of what she was to expect in Lady Catherine de Bourgh, and trusting their opinion of her—their opinion of everybody—would always coincide, there was a solicitude, an interest, which she felt must ever attach her to him with a most sincere regard; and she parted from him convinced that, whether married or single, he must always be her model of the amiable and pleasing.

Her fellow-travellers the next day were not of a kind to make her think him less agreeable. Sir William Lucas, and his daughter Maria, a good-humoured girl, but as empty-headed as himself, had nothing to say that could be worth

hearing, and were listened to with about as much
delight as the rattle of the chaise. Elizabeth
loved absurdities, but she had known Sir
William's too long. He could tell her nothing
new of the wonders of his presentation and
knighthood ; and his civilities were worn out,
like his information.

It was a journey of only twenty-four miles,
and they began it so early as to be in Gracechurch Street by noon. As they drove to Mr.
Gardiner's door, Jane was at a drawing-room
window watching their arrival ; when they
entered the passage she was there to welcome
them, and Elizabeth, looking earnestly in her
face, was pleased to see it healthful and lovely
as ever. On the stairs were a troop of little
boys and girls, whose eagerness for their cousin's
appearance would not allow them to wait in the
drawing-room, and whose shyness, as they had
not seen her for a twelvemonth, prevented their
coming lower. All was joy and kindness. The
day passed most pleasantly away : the morning
in bustle and shopping, and the evening at one
of the theatres.

Elizabeth then contrived to sit by her aunt.
Their first subject was her sister ; and she was
more grieved than astonished to hear, in reply to
her minute inquiries, that though Jane always
struggled to support her spirits, there were

periods of dejection. It was reasonable, however, to hope that they would not continue long. Mrs. Gardiner gave her the particulars also of Miss Bingley's visit in Gracechurch Street, and repeated conversations occurring at different times between Jane and herself, which proved that the former had, from her heart, given up the acquaintance.

Mrs. Gardiner then rallied her niece on Wickham's desertion, and complimented her on bearing it so well.

'But, my dear Elizabeth,' she added, 'what sort of girl is Miss King? I should be sorry to think our friend mercenary.'

'Pray, my dear aunt, what is the difference in matrimonial affairs between the mercenary and the prudent motive? Where does discretion end, and avarice begin? Last Christmas you were afraid of his marrying me, because it would be imprudent; and now, because he is trying to get a girl with only ten thousand pounds, you want to find out that he is mercenary.'

'If you will only tell me what sort of girl Miss King is, I shall know what to think.'

'She is a very good kind of girl, I believe. I know no harm of her.'

'But he paid her not the smallest attention till her grandfather's death made her mistress of this fortune.'

'No—why should he? If it were not allowable for him to gain *my* affections because I had no money, what occasion could there be for making love to a girl whom he did not care about, and who was equally poor?'

'But there seems indelicacy in directing his attention towards her so soon after this event.'

'A man in distressed circumstances has not time for all those elegant decorums which other people may observe. If *she* does not object to it, why should *we*?'

'*Her* not objecting does not justify *him*. It only shews her being deficient in something herself—sense or feeling.'

'Well,' cried Elizabeth, 'have it as you chuse. *He* shall be mercenary, and *she* shall be foolish.'

'No, Lizzy, that is what I do *not* chuse. I should be sorry, you know, to think ill of a young man who has lived so long in Derbyshire.'

'Oh! if that is all, I have a very poor opinion of young men who live in Derbyshire; and their intimate friends who live in Hertfordshire are not much better. I am sick of them all. Thank Heaven! I am going to-morrow where I shall find a man who has not one agreeable quality, who has neither manner nor sense to recommend him. Stupid men are the only ones worth knowing, after all.'

232

'Take care, Lizzy; that speech savours strongly of disappointment.'

Before they were separated by the conclusion of the play, she had the unexpected happiness of an invitation to accompany her uncle and aunt in a tour of pleasure which they proposed taking in the summer.

'We have not quite determined how far it shall carry us,' said Mrs. Gardiner, 'but, perhaps, to the Lakes.'

No scheme could have been more agreeable to Elizabeth, and her acceptance of the invitation was most ready and grateful. 'My dear, dear aunt,' she rapturously cried, 'what delight! what felicity! You give me fresh life and vigour. Adieu to disappointment and spleen. What are men to rocks and mountains? Oh! what hours of transport we shall spend! And when we *do* return, it shall not be like other travellers, without being able to give one accurate idea of anything. We *will* know where we have gone —we *will* recollect what we have seen. Lakes, mountains, and rivers shall not be jumbled together in our imaginations; nor, when we attempt to describe any particular scene, will we begin quarrelling about its relative situation. Let *our* first effusions be less insupportable than those of the generality of travellers.'

CHAPTER XXVIII

EVERY object in the next day's journey was new and interesting to Elizabeth; and her spirits were in a state of enjoyment; for she had seen her sister looking so well as to banish all fear for her health, and the prospect of her northern tour was a constant source of delight.

When they left the highroad for the lane to Hunsford, every eye was in search of the Parsonage, and every turning expected to bring it in view. The paling of Rosings Park was their boundary on one side. Elizabeth smiled at the recollection of all that she had heard of its inhabitants.

At length the Parsonage was discernible. The garden sloping to the road, the house standing in it, the green pales, and the laurel hedge, everything declared they were arriving. Mr. Collins and Charlotte appeared at the door, and the carriage stopped at the small gate which led by a short gravel walk to the house amidst the nods and smiles of the whole party. In a moment they were all out of the chaise, rejoicing

234

at the sight of each other. Mrs. Collins welcomed her friend with the liveliest pleasure, and Elizabeth was more and more satisfied with coming when she found herself so affectionately received. She saw instantly that her cousin's manners were not altered by his marriage: his formal civility was just what it had been, and he detained her some minutes at the gate to hear and satisfy his inquiries after all her family. They were then, with no other delay than his pointing out the neatness of the entrance, taken into the house; and as soon as they were in the parlour he welcomed them a second time, with ostentatious formality, to his humble abode, and punctually repeated all his wife's offers of refreshment.

Elizabeth was prepared to see him in his glory; and she could not help fancying that in displaying the good proportion of the room, its aspect and its furniture, he addressed himself particularly to her, as if wishing to make her feel what she had lost in refusing him. But though everything seemed neat and comfortable, she was not able to gratify him by any sigh of repentance, and rather looked with wonder at her friend that she could have so cheerful an air with such a companion. When Mr. Collins said anything of which his wife might reasonably be ashamed, which certainly was not unseldom, she involun-

tarily turned her eye on Charlotte. Once or
twice she could discern a faint blush ; but in
general Charlotte wisely did not hear. After
sitting long enough to admire every article of
furniture in the room, from the sideboard to the
fender, to give an account of their journey, and
of all that had happened in London, Mr. Collins
invited them to take a stroll in the garden,
which was large and well laid out, and to the
cultivation of which he attended himself. To
work in his garden was one of his most respectable pleasures ; and Elizabeth admired the command of countenance with which Charlotte talked
of the healthfulness of the exercise, and owned
she encouraged it as much as possible. Here,
leading the way through every walk and cross-
walk, and scarcely allowing them an interval to
utter the praises he asked for, every view was
pointed out with a minuteness which left beauty
entirely behind. He could number the fields
in every direction, and could tell how many
trees there were in the most distant clump.
But of all the views which his garden, or which
the country or the kingdom could boast, none
were to be compared with the prospect of
Rosings, afforded by an opening in the trees
that bordered the park nearly opposite the front
of his house. It was a handsome modern build-
ing, well situated on rising ground.

From his garden Mr. Collins would have led them round his two meadows; but the ladies, not having shoes to encounter the remains of a white frost, turned back; and while Sir William accompanied him, Charlotte took her sister and friend over the house, extremely well pleased, probably, to have the opportunity of shewing it without her husband's help. It was rather small, but well built and convenient; and everything was fitted up and arranged with a neatness and consistency of which Elizabeth gave Charlotte all the credit. When Mr. Collins could be forgotten, there was really a great air of comfort throughout, and by Charlotte's evident enjoyment of it, Elizabeth supposed he must be often forgotten.

She had already learnt that Lady Catherine was still in the country. It was spoken of again while they were at dinner, when Mr. Collins joining in, observed—

'Yes, Miss Elizabeth, you will have the honour of seeing Lady Catherine de Bourgh on the ensuing Sunday at church, and I need not say you will be delighted with her. She is all affability and condescension, and I doubt not but you will be honoured with some portion of her notice when service is over. I have scarcely any hesitation in saying that she will include you and my sister Maria in every invita-

tion with which she honours us during your stay
here. Her behaviour to my dear Charlotte is
charming. We dine at Rosings twice every
week, and are never allowed to walk home.
Her ladyship's carriage is regularly ordered for
us. I *should* say, one of her ladyship's carriages,
for she has several.'

'Lady Catherine is a very respectable, sensible
woman indeed,' added Charlotte, 'and a most
attentive neighbour.'

'Very true, my dear, that is exactly what I
say. She is the sort of woman whom one cannot
regard with too much deference.'

The evening was spent chiefly in talking over
Hertfordshire news, and telling again what had
been already written; and when it closed,
Elizabeth, in the solitude of her chamber, had
to meditate upon Charlotte's degree of contentment, to understand her address in guiding, and
composure in bearing with, her husband, and to
acknowledge that it was all done very well.
She had also to anticipate how her visit would
pass, the quiet tenour of their usual employments, the vexatious interruptions of Mr. Collins,
and the gaieties of their intercourse with Rosings.
A lively imagination soon settled it all.

About the middle of the next day, as she was
in her room getting ready for a walk, a sudden
noise below seemed to speak the whole house in

confusion; and, after listening a moment, she heard somebody running upstairs in a violent hurry, and calling loudly after her. She opened the door and met Maria in the landing-place, who, breathless with agitation, cried out—

'Oh, my dear Eliza! pray make haste and come into the dining-room, for there is such a sight to be seen! I will not tell you what it is. Make haste, and come down this moment.'

Elizabeth asked questions in vain: Maria would tell her nothing more, and down they ran into the dining-room, which fronted the lane, in quest of this wonder! it was two ladies stopping in a low phaeton at the garden gate.

'And is this all?' cried Elizabeth. 'I expected at least that the pigs were got into the garden, and here is nothing but Lady Catherine and her daughter!'

'La! my dear,' said Maria, quite shocked at the mistake, 'it is not Lady Catherine. The old lady is Mrs. Jenkinson, who lives with them; the other is Miss de Bourgh. Only look at her. She is quite a little creature. Who would have thought she could be so thin and small!'

'She is abominably rude to keep Charlotte out of doors in all this wind. Why does she not come in?'

'Oh, Charlotte says she hardly ever does. It

is the greatest of favours when Miss de Bourgh comes in.'

'I like her appearance,' said Elizabeth, struck with other ideas. 'She looks sickly and cross. Yes, she will do for him very well. She will make him a very proper wife.'

Mr. Collins and Charlotte were both standing at the gate in conversation with the ladies; and Sir William, to Elizabeth's high diversion, was stationed in the doorway, in earnest contemplation of the greatness before him, and constantly bowing whenever Miss de Bourgh looked that way.

At length there was nothing more to be said; the ladies drove on, and the others returned into the house. Mr. Collins no sooner saw the two girls than he began to congratulate them on their good fortune, which Charlotte explained by letting them know that the whole party was asked to dine at Rosings the next day.

CHAPTER XXIX

Mr. Collins's triumph, in consequence of this invitation, was complete. The power of displaying the grandeur of his patroness to his wondering visitors, and of letting them see her civility towards himself and his wife, was exactly what he had wished for; and that an opportunity of doing it should be given so soon, was such an instance of Lady Catherine's condescension, as he knew not how to admire enough.

'I confess,' said he, 'that I should not have been at all surprised by her ladyship's asking us on Sunday to drink tea and spend the evening at Rosings. I rather expected, from my knowledge of her affability, that it would happen. But who could have foreseen such an attention as this? Who could have imagined that we should receive an invitation to dine there (an invitation, moreover, including the whole party) so immediately after your arrival!'

'I am the less surprised at what has happened,' replied Sir William, 'from that knowledge of what the manners of the great really are, which

my situation in life has allowed me to acquire.
About the court such instances of elegant
breeding are not uncommon.'

Scarcely anything was talked of the whole
day or next morning but their visit to Rosings.
Mr. Collins was carefully instructing them in
what they were to expect, that the sight of
such rooms, so many servants, and so splendid
a dinner, might not wholly overpower them.

When the ladies were separating for the
toilette, he said to Elizabeth—

'Do not make yourself uneasy, my dear
cousin, about your apparel. Lady Catherine
is far from requiring that elegance of dress in
us which becomes herself and daughter. I
would advise you merely to put on whatever of
your clothes is superior to the rest—there is no
occasion for anything more. Lady Catherine
will not think the worse of you for being simply
dressed. She likes to have the distinction of
rank preserved.'

While they were dressing, he came two or
three times to their different doors, to recommend their being quick, as Lady Catherine very
much objected to be kept waiting for her dinner.
Such formidable accounts of her ladyship, and
her manner of living, quite frightened Maria
Lucas, who had been little used to company,
and she looked forward to her introduction

at Rosings with as much apprehension as her father had done to his presentation at St. James's.

As the weather was fine they had a pleasant walk of about half a mile across the park. Every park has its beauty and its prospects; and Elizabeth saw much to be pleased with, though she could not be in such raptures as Mr. Collins expected the scene to inspire, and was but slightly affected by his enumeration of the windows in front of the house, and his relation of what the glazing altogether had originally cost Sir Lewis de Bourgh.

When they ascended the steps to the hall, Maria's alarm was every moment increasing, and even Sir William did not look perfectly calm. Elizabeth's courage did not fail her. She had heard nothing of Lady Catherine that spoke her awful from any extraordinary talents or miraculous virtue, and the mere stateliness of money and rank she thought she could witness without trepidation.

From the entrance-hall, of which Mr. Collins pointed out, with a rapturous air, the fine proportion and finished ornaments, they followed the servants through an antechamber, to the room where Lady Catherine, her daughter, and Mrs. Jenkinson were sitting. Her ladyship, with great condescension, arose to receive them;

PRIDE AND PREJUDICE

and as Mrs. Collins had settled it with her husband that the office of introduction should be
hers, it was performed in a proper manner,
without any of those apologies and thanks
which he would have thought necessary.

In spite of having been at St. James's, Sir
William was so completely awed by the grandeur
surrounding him, that he had but just courage
enough to make a very low bow, and take his
seat without saying a word; and his daughter,
frightened almost out of her senses, sat on the
edge of her chair, not knowing which way to
look. Elizabeth found herself quite equal to
the scene, and could observe the three ladies
before her composedly.—Lady Catherine was a
tall, large woman, with strongly marked features,
which might once have been handsome. Her
air was not conciliating, nor was her manner of
receiving them such as to make her visitors
forget their inferior rank. She was not rendered
formidable by silence; but whatever she said
was spoken in so authoritative a tone as marked
her self-importance, and brought Mr. Wickham
immediately to Elizabeth's mind; and from the
observation of the day altogether, she believed
Lady Catherine to be exactly what he had represented.

When, after examining the mother, in whose
countenance and deportment she soon found

some resemblance of Mr. Darcy, she turned her eyes on the daughter, she could almost have joined in Maria's astonishment at her being so thin and so small. There was neither in figure nor face any likeness between the ladies. Miss de Bourgh was pale and sickly; her features, though not plain, were insignificant; and she spoke very little, except in a low voice to Mrs. Jenkinson, in whose appearance there was nothing remarkable, and who was entirely engaged in listening to what she said, and placing a screen in the proper direction before her eyes.

After sitting a few minutes they were all sent to one of the windows to admire the view, Mr. Collins attending them to point out its beauties, and Lady Catherine kindly informing them that it was much better worth looking at in the summer.

The dinner was exceedingly handsome, and there were all the servants and all the articles of plate which Mr. Collins had promised; and, as he had likewise foretold, he took his seat at the bottom of the table, by her ladyship's desire, and looked as if he felt that life could furnish nothing greater. He carved, and ate, and praised with delighted alacrity; and every dish was commended, first by him and then by Sir William, who was now enough recovered to echo whatever his son-in-law said, in a manner which Elizabeth wondered Lady Catherine could bear. But Lady Catherine seemed gratified by their excessive admiration, and gave most gracious smiles, especially when any dish on the table proved a novelty to them. The party did not supply much conversation. Elizabeth was ready to speak whenever there was an opening, but she was seated between Charlotte and Miss de Bourgh—the former of whom was engaged in listening to Lady Catherine, and the latter said not a word to her all dinner-time. Mrs. Jenkinson was chiefly employed in watching how little Miss de Bourgh ate, pressing her to try some other dish, and fearing she was indisposed. Maria thought speaking out of the question, and the gentlemen did nothing but eat and admire.

When the ladies returned to the drawing-room, there was little to be done but to hear Lady Catherine talk, which she did without any intermission till coffee came in, delivering her opinion on every subject in so decisive a manner as proved that she was not used to have her judgment controverted. She inquired into Charlotte's domestic concerns familiarly and minutely, and gave her a great deal of advice as to the management of them all; told her how everything ought to be regulated in so small a family as hers, and instructed her as to the care of her

246

cows and her poultry. Elizabeth found that
nothing was beneath this great lady's attention,
which could furnish her with an occasion of
dictating to others. In the intervals of her
discourse with Mrs. Collins she addressed a
variety of questions to Maria and Elizabeth, but
especially to the latter, of whose connexions
she knew the least, and who, she observed to
Mrs. Collins, was a very genteel, pretty kind of
girl. She asked her, at different times, how
many sisters she had, whether they were older
or younger than herself, whether any of them
were likely to be married, whether they were
handsome, where they had been educated,
what carriage her father kept, and what had
been her mother's maiden name? Elizabeth
felt all the impertinence of her questions,
but answered them very composedly. Lady
Catherine then observed—

'Your father's estate is entailed on Mr. Collins,
I think. For your sake,' turning to Charlotte,
'I am glad of it; but otherwise I see no occa-
sion for entailing estates from the female line.
It was not thought necessary in Sir Lewis de
Bourgh's family. Do you play and sing, Miss
Bennet?'

'A little.'

'Oh! then—some time or other we shall
be happy to hear you. Our instrument is a

capital one, probably superior to—— You shall
try it some day. Do your sisters play and
sing?'

'One of them does.'

'Why did not you all learn? You ought all
to have learned. The Miss Webbs all play, and
their father has not so good an income as yours.
Do you draw?'

'No, not at all.'

'What, none of you?'

'Not one.'

'That is very strange. But I suppose you
had no opportunity. Your mother should have
taken you to town every spring for the benefit
of masters.'

'My mother would have had no objection,
but my father hates London.'

'Has your governess left you?'

'We never had any governess.'

'No governess! How was that possible?
Five daughters brought up at home without a
governess! I never heard of such a thing.
Your mother must have been quite a slave to
your education.'

Elizabeth could hardly help smiling as she
assured her that had not been the case.

'Then, who taught you? who attended to
you? Without a governess, you must have
been neglected.'

248

' Compared with some families, I believe we were; but such of us as wished to learn never wanted the means. We were always encouraged to read, and had all the masters that were necessary. Those who chose to be idle, certainly might.'

' Ay, no doubt; but that is what a governess will prevent, and if I had known your mother, I should have advised her most strenuously to engage one. I always say that nothing is to be done in education without steady and regular instruction, and nobody but a governess can give it. It is wonderful how many families I have been the means of supplying in that way. I am always glad to get a young person well placed out. Four nieces of Mrs. Jenkinson are most delightfully situated through my means; and it was but the other day that I recommended another young person, who was merely accidentally mentioned to me, and the family are quite delighted with her. Mrs. Collins, did I tell you of Lady Metcalfe's calling yesterday to thank me? She finds Miss Pope a treasure. "Lady Catherine," said she, "you have given me a treasure." Are any of your younger sisters out, Miss Bennet?'

' Yes, ma'am, all.'

' All!—What, all five out at once? Very odd!—And you only the second. The younger ones out before the elder are married! Your younger sisters must be very young?'

'Yes, my youngest is not sixteen. Perhaps *she* is full young to be much in company. But really, ma'am, I think it would be very hard upon younger sisters, that they should not have their share of society and amusement, because the elder may not have the means or inclination to marry early. The last-born has as good a right to the pleasures of youth as the first. And to be kept back on *such* a motive! I think it would not be very likely to promote sisterly affection or delicacy of mind.'

'Upon my word,' said her ladyship, 'you give your opinion very decidedly for so young a person. Pray, what is your age?'

'With three younger sisters grown up,' replied Elizabeth, smiling, 'your ladyship can hardly expect me to own it.'

Lady Catherine seemed quite astonished at not receiving a direct answer; and Elizabeth suspected herself to be the first creature who had ever dared to trifle with so much dignified impertinence.

'You cannot be more than twenty, I am sure, therefore you need not conceal your age.'

'I am not one-and-twenty.'

When the gentlemen had joined them, and tea was over, the card-tables were placed. Lady

Catherine, Sir William, and Mr. and Mrs. Collins sat down to quadrille; and as Miss de Bourgh chose to play at cassino, the two girls had the honour of assisting Mrs. Jenkinson to make up her party. Their table was superlatively stupid. Scarcely a syllable was uttered that did not relate to the game, except when Mrs. Jenkinson expressed her fears of Miss de Bourgh's being too hot or too cold, or having too much or too little light. A great deal more passed at the other table. Lady Catherine was generally speaking—stating the mistakes of the three others, or relating some anecdote of herself. Mr. Collins was employed in agreeing to every-thing her ladyship said, thanking her for every fish he won, and apologising if he thought he won too many. Sir William did not say much. He was storing his memory with anecdotes and noble names.

When Lady Catherine and her daughter had played as long as they chose, the tables were broken up, the carriage was offered to Mrs. Collins, gratefully accepted, and immediately ordered. The party then gathered round the fire to hear Lady Catherine determine what weather they were to have on the morrow. From these instructions they were summoned by the arrival of the coach; and with many speeches of thankfulness on Mr. Collins's side, and as many bows on Sir William's, they departed. As soon as they had driven from the door, Elizabeth was called on by her cousin to give her opinion of all that she had seen at Rosings, which, for Charlotte's sake, she made more favourable than it really was. But her commendation, though costing her some trouble, could by no mean satisfy Mr. Collins, and he was very soon obliged to take her ladyship's praise into his own hands.

CHAPTER XXX

SIR WILLIAM stayed only a week at Hunsford, but his visit was long enough to convince him of his daughter's being most comfortably settled, and of her possessing such a husband and such a neighbour as were not often met with. While Sir William was with them Mr. Collins devoted his mornings to driving him out in his gig, and shewing him the country; but when he went away, the whole family returned to their usual employments, and Elizabeth was thankful to find that they did not see more of her cousin by the alteration, for the chief of the time between breakfast and dinner was now passed by him either at work in the garden, or in reading and writing, and looking out of window in his own book-room, which fronted the road. The room in which the ladies sat was backwards. Elizabeth at first had rather wondered that Charlotte should not prefer the dining-parlour for common use; it was a better-sized room, and had a pleasanter aspect; but she soon saw that her friend had an excellent reason for what

253

she did, for Mr. Collins would undoubtedly have been much less in his own apartment had they sat in one equally lively; and she gave Charlotte credit for the arrangement.

From the drawing-room they could distinguish nothing in the lane, and were indebted to Mr. Collins for the knowledge of what carriages went along, and how often especially Miss de Bourgh drove by in her phaeton, which he never failed coming to inform them of, though it happened almost every day. She not unfrequently stopped at the Parsonage, and had a few minutes' conversation with Charlotte, but was scarcely ever prevailed on to get out.

Very few days passed in which Mr. Collins did not walk to Rosings, and not many in which his wife did not think it necessary to go likewise; and till Elizabeth recollected that there might be other family livings to be disposed of, she could not understand the sacrifice of so many hours. Now and then they were honoured with a call from her ladyship, and nothing escaped her observation that was passing in the room during these visits. She examined into their employments, looked at their work, and advised them to do it differently; found fault with the arrangement of the furniture, or detected the housemaid in negligence; and if she accepted any refreshment, seemed to do it only

254

for the sake of finding out that Mrs. Collins's joints of meat were too large for her family.

Elizabeth soon perceived that, though this great lady was not in the commission of the peace for the county, she was a most active magistrate in her own parish, the minutest concerns of which were carried to her by Mr. Collins; and whenever any of the cottagers were disposed to be quarrelsome, discontented, or too poor, she sallied forth into the village to settle their differences, silence their complaints, and scold them into harmony and plenty.

The entertainment of dining at Rosings was repeated about twice a week; and, allowing for the loss of Sir William, and there being only one card-table in the evening, every such entertainment was the counterpart of the first. Their other engagements were few, as the style of living of the neighbourhood in general was beyond the Collinses' reach. This, however, was no evil to Elizabeth, and upon the whole she spent her time comfortably enough; there were half-hours of pleasant conversation with Charlotte, and the weather was so fine for the time of year that she had often great enjoyment out of doors. Her favourite walk, and where she frequently went while the others were calling on Lady Catherine, was along the open grove which edged that side of the park, where there was a nice sheltered path, which no one seemed to value but herself, and where she felt beyond the reach of Lady Catherine's curiosity.

In this quiet way the first fortnight of her visit soon passed away. Easter was approaching, and the week preceding it was to bring an addition to the family at Rosings, which in so small a circle must be important. Elizabeth had heard soon after her arrival that Mr. Darcy was expected there in the course of a few weeks, and though there were not many of her acquaintance whom she did not prefer, his coming would furnish one comparatively new to look at in their Rosings parties, and she might be amused in seeing how hopeless Miss Bingley's designs on him were, by his behaviour to his cousin, for whom he was evidently destined by Lady Catherine, who talked of his coming with the greatest satisfaction, spoke of him in terms of the highest admiration, and seemed almost angry to find that he had already been frequently seen by Miss Lucas and herself.

His arrival was soon known at the Parsonage; for Mr. Collins was walking the whole morning within view of the lodges opening into Hunsford Lane, in order to have the earliest assurance of it; and after making his bow as the carriage turned into the Park, hurried home with the great intelligence. On the following morning he hastened to Rosings to pay his respects. There were two nephews of Lady Catherine to require them, for Mr. Darcy had brought with him a Colonel Fitzwilliam, the younger son of his uncle, Lord ——, and to the great surprise of all the party, when Mr. Collins returned, the gentlemen accompanied him. Charlotte had seen them from her husband's room crossing the road, and immediately running into the other, told the girls what an honour they might expect, adding—

'I may thank you, Eliza, for this piece of civility. Mr. Darcy would never have come so soon to wait upon me.'

Elizabeth had scarcely time to disclaim all right to the compliment before their approach was announced by the door-bell, and shortly afterwards the three gentlemen entered the room. Colonel Fitzwilliam, who led the way, was about thirty, not handsome, but in person and address most truly the gentleman. Mr. Darcy looked just as he had been used to look in Hertfordshire—paid his compliments, with his usual reserve, to Mrs. Collins, and whatever might be his feelings towards her friend, met her with every appearance of composure. Elizabeth merely curtseyed to him, without saying a word.

Colonel Fitzwilliam entered into conversation directly with the readiness and ease of a well-bred man, and talked very pleasantly ; but his cousin, after having addressed a slight observation on the house and garden to Mrs. Collins, sat for some time without speaking to anybody. At length, however, his civility was so far awakened as to inquire of Elizabeth after the health of her family. She answered him in the usual way, and after a moment's pause, added—

'My eldest sister has been in town these three months. Have you never happened to see her there ?'

She was perfectly sensible that he never had ; but she wished to see whether he would betray any consciousness of what had passed between the Bingleys and Jane, and she thought he looked a little confused as he answered that he had never been so fortunate as to meet Miss Bennet. The subject was pursued no farther, and the gentlemen soon afterwards went away.

CHAPTER XXXI

COLONEL FITZWILLIAM's manners were very much admired at the Parsonage, and the ladies all felt that he must add considerably to the pleasure of their engagements at Rosings. It was some days, however, before they received any invitation thither — for while there were visitors in the house they could not be necessary; and it was not till Easter-day, almost a week after the gentlemen's arrival, that they were honoured by such an attention, and then they were merely asked on leaving church to come there in the evening. For the last week they had seen very little of either Lady Catherine or her daughter. Colonel Fitzwilliam had called at the Parsonage more than once during the time, but Mr. Darcy they had only seen at church.

The invitation was accepted of course, and at a proper hour they joined the party in Lady Catherine's drawing-room. Her ladyship received them civilly, but it was plain that their company was by no means so acceptable as

259

when she could get nobody else; and she was, in fact, almost engrossed by her nephews, speaking to them, especially to Darcy, much more than to any other person in the room.

Colonel Fitzwilliam seemed really glad to see them; anything was a welcome relief to him at Rosings; and Mrs. Collins's pretty friend had moreover caught his fancy very much. He now seated himself by her, and talked so agreeably of Kent and Hertfordshire, of travelling and staying at home, of new books and music, that Elizabeth had never been half so well entertained in that room before; and they conversed with so much spirit and flow, as to draw the attention of Lady Catherine herself, as well as of Mr. Darcy. *His* eyes had been soon and repeatedly turned towards them with a look of curiosity; and that her ladyship, after a while, shared the feeling, was more openly acknowledged, for she did not scruple to call out—

'What is that you are saying, Fitzwilliam? What is it you are talking of? What are you telling Miss Bennet? Let me hear what it is.'

'We are speaking of music, madam,' said he, when no longer able to avoid a reply.

'Of music! Then pray speak aloud. It is of all subjects my delight. I must have my

share in the conversation if you are speaking
of music. There are few people in England,
I suppose, who have more true enjoyment of
music than myself, or a better natural taste.
If I had ever learnt, I should have been a great
proficient. And so would Anne, if her health
had allowed her to apply. I am confident that
she would have performed delightfully. How
does Georgiana get on, Darcy ?'

Mr. Darcy spoke with affectionate praise of
his sister's proficiency.

'I am very glad to hear such a good account
of her,' said Lady Catherine ; 'and pray tell her
from me, that she cannot expect to excel if she
does not practise a great deal.'

'I assure you, madam,' he replied, 'that she
does not need such advice. She practises very
constantly.'

'So much the better. It cannot be done too
much ; and when I next write to her, I shall
charge her not to neglect it on any account.
I often tell young ladies that no excellence
in music is to be acquired without constant
practice. I have told Miss Bennet several times
that she will never play really well unless she
practises more ; and though Mrs. Collins has no
instrument, she is very welcome, as I have often
told her, to come to Rosings every day, and
play on the pianoforte in Mrs. Jenkinson's room.

She would be in nobody's way, you know, in that part of the house.'

Mr. Darcy looked a little ashamed of his aunt's ill-breeding, and made no answer.

When coffee was over Colonel Fitzwilliam reminded Elizabeth of having promised to play to him; and she sat down directly to the instrument. He drew a chair near her. Lady Catherine listened to half a song, and then talked, as before, to her other nephew; till the latter walked away from her, and moving with his usual deliberation towards the pianoforte, stationed himself so as to command a full view of the fair performer's countenance. Elizabeth saw what he was doing, and at the first convenient pause, turned to him with an arch smile, and said—

'You mean to frighten me, Mr. Darcy, by coming in all this state to hear me? But I will not be alarmed though your sister *does* play so well. There is a stubbornness about me that never can bear to be frightened at the will of others. My courage always rises with every attempt to intimidate me.'

'I shall not say that you are mistaken,' he replied, 'because you could not really believe me to entertain any design of alarming you; and I have had the pleasure of your acquaintance long enough to know that you find great enjoyment in occasionally professing opinions which in fact are not your own.'

Elizabeth laughed heartily at this picture of herself, and said to Colonel Fitzwilliam, 'Your cousin will give you a very pretty notion of me, and teach you not to believe a word I say. I am particularly unlucky in meeting with a person so well able to expose my real character, in a part of the world where I had hoped to pass myself off with some degree of credit. Indeed, Mr. Darcy, it is very ungenerous in you to mention all that you knew to my disadvantage in Hertfordshire—and, give me leave to say, very impolitic too—for it is provoking me to retaliate, and such things may come out as will shock your relations to hear.'

'I am not afraid of you,' said he smilingly.

'Pray let me hear what you have to accuse him of,' cried Colonel Fitzwilliam. 'I should like to know how he behaves among strangers.'

'You shall hear then—but prepare yourself for something very dreadful. The first time of my ever seeing him in Hertfordshire, you must know, was at a ball—and at this ball, what do you think he did? He danced only four dances! I am sorry to pain you—but so it was. He danced only four dances, though gentlemen were scarce; and, to my certain knowledge, more than one young lady was sitting down in want of a partner. Mr. Darcy, you cannot deny the fact.'

'I had not at that time the honour of knowing any lady in the assembly beyond my own party.'

'True; and nobody can ever be introduced in a ballroom. Well, Colonel Fitzwilliam, what do I play next? My fingers wait your orders.'

'Perhaps,' said Darcy, 'I should have judged better had I sought an introduction; but I am ill qualified to recommend myself to strangers.'

'Shall we ask your cousin the reason of this?' said Elizabeth, still addressing Colonel Fitzwilliam. 'Shall we ask him why a man of sense and education, and who has lived in the world, is ill qualified to recommend himself to strangers?'

'I can answer your question,' said Fitzwilliam, 'without applying to him. It is because he will not give himself the trouble.'

'I certainly have not the talent which some people possess,' said Darcy, 'of conversing easily with those I have never seen before. I cannot catch their tone of conversation, or appear interested in their concerns, as I often see done.'

'My fingers,' said Elizabeth, 'do not move over this instrument in the masterly manner which I see so many women's do. They have not the same force or rapidity, and do not produce the same expression. But then I have always supposed it to be my own fault—because I would not take the trouble of practising. It is not that I do not believe *my* fingers as capable as any other woman's of superior execution.'

Darcy smiled and said, 'You are perfectly right. You have employed your time much better. No one admitted to the privilege of hearing you can think anything wanting. We neither of us perform to strangers.'

Here they were interrupted by Lady Catherine, who called out to know what they were talking of. Elizabeth immediately began playing again. Lady Catherine approached, and, after listening for a few minutes, said to Darcy—

'Miss Bennet would not play at all amiss if she practised more, and could have the advantage of a London master. She has a very good notion of fingering, though her taste is not equal to Anne's. Anne would have been a delightful performer, had her health allowed her to learn.'

Elizabeth looked at Darcy to see how cordially he assented to his cousin's praise; but neither at that moment nor at any other could she discern any symptom of love; and from the whole of his behaviour to Miss de Bourgh she derived this comfort for Miss Bingley, that he might

have been just as likely to marry *her*, had she
been his relation.

Lady Catherine continued her remarks on
Elizabeth's performance, mixing with them
many instructions on execution and taste.
Elizabeth received them with all the forbearance
of civility, and, at the request of the gentlemen,
remained at the instrument till her ladyship's
carriage was ready to take them all home.

CHAPTER XXXII

ELIZABETH was sitting by herself the next morning, and writing to Jane, while Mrs. Collins and Maria were gone on business into the village, when she was startled by a ring at the door, the certain signal of a visitor. As she had heard no carriage, she thought it not unlikely to be Lady Catherine, and under that apprehension was putting away her half-finished letter that she might escape all impertinent questions, when the door opened, and to her very great surprise Mr. Darcy, and Mr. Darcy only, entered the room.

He seemed astonished too on finding her alone, and apologised for his intrusion by letting her know that he had understood all the ladies to be within.

They then sat down, and when her inquiries after Rosings were made, seemed in danger of sinking into total silence. It was absolutely necessary, therefore, to think of something, and in this emergence, recollecting *when* she had seen him last in Hertfordshire, and feeling curious to

267

know what he would say on the subject of their
hasty departure, she observed—

'How very suddenly you all quitted Netherfield last November, Mr. Darcy! It must have
been a most agreeable surprise to Mr. Bingley
to see you all after him so soon; for, if I recollect right, he went but the day before. He
and his sisters were well, I hope, when you left
London?'

'Perfectly so, I thank you.'

She found that she was to receive no other
answer, and, after a short pause, added—

'I think I have understood that Mr. Bingley
has not much idea of ever returning to Netherfield again?'

'I have never heard him say so; but it is
probable that he may spend very little of his
time there in future. He has many friends,
and he is at a time of life when friends and
engagements are continually increasing.'

'If he means to be but little at Netherfield,
it would be better for the neighbourhood that
he should give up the place entirely, for then
we might possibly get a settled family there.
But, perhaps, Mr. Bingley did not take the
house so much for the convenience of the neighbourhood as for his own, and we must expect
him to keep or quit it on the same principle.'

'I should not be surprised,' said Darcy, 'if

he were to give it up as soon as any eligible purchase offers.'

Elizabeth made no answer. She was afraid of talking longer of his friend; and, having nothing else to say, was now determined to leave the trouble of finding a subject to him.

He took the hint, and soon began with, 'This seems a very comfortable house. Lady Catherine, I believe, did a great deal to it when Mr. Collins first came to Hunsford.'

'I believe she did—and I am sure she could not have bestowed her kindness on a more grateful object.'

'Mr. Collins appears very fortunate in his choice of a wife.'

'Yes, indeed; his friends may well rejoice in his having met with one of the very few sensible women who would have accepted him, or have made him happy if they had. My friend has an excellent understanding—though I am not certain that I consider her marrying Mr. Collins as the wisest thing she ever did. She seems perfectly happy, however, and in a prudential light it is certainly a very good match for her.'

'It must be very agreeable to her to be settled within so easy a distance of her own family and friends.'

'An easy distance, do you call it? It is nearly fifty miles.'

269

'And what is fifty miles of good road? Little more than half a day's journey. Yes, I call it a very easy distance.'

'I should never have considered the distance as one of the *advantages* of the match,' cried Elizabeth. 'I should never have said Mrs. Collins was settled *near* her family.'

'It is a proof of your own attachment to Hertfordshire. Anything beyond the very neighbourhood of Longbourn, I suppose, would appear far.'

As he spoke there was a sort of smile which Elizabeth fancied she understood; he must be supposing her to be thinking of Jane and Netherfield, and she blushed as she answered—

'I do not mean to say that a woman may not be settled too near her family. The far and the near must be relative, and depend on many varying circumstances. Where there is fortune to make the expenses of travelling unimportant, distance becomes no evil. But that is not the case *here*. Mr. and Mrs. Collins have a comfortable income, but not such a one as will allow of frequent journeys—and I am persuaded my friend would not call herself *near* her family under less than *half* the present distance.'

Mr. Darcy drew his chair a little towards her, and said, '*You* cannot have a right to such very strong local attachment. *You* cannot have been always at Longbourn.'

Elizabeth looked surprised. The gentleman experienced some change of feeling; he drew back his chair, took a newspaper from the table, and, glancing over it, said, in a colder voice—

'Are you pleased with Kent?'

A short dialogue on the subject of the county ensued, on either side calm and concise—and soon put an end to by the entrance of Charlotte and her sister, just returned from their walk. The *tête-à-tête* surprised them. Mr. Darcy related the mistake which had occasioned his intruding on Miss Bennet, and after sitting a few minutes longer without saying much to anybody, went away.

'What can be the meaning of this?' said Charlotte, as soon as he was gone. 'My dear Eliza, he must be in love with you, or he would never have called on us in this familiar way.'

But when Elizabeth told of his silence, it did not seem very likely, even to Charlotte's wishes, to be the case; and after various conjectures, they could at last only suppose his visit to proceed from the difficulty of finding anything to do, which was the more probable from the time of year. All field sports were over. Within doors there was Lady Catherine, books, and a billiard-table, but gentlemen cannot be always within doors; and in the nearness of the Parsonage, or the pleasantness of the walk to it, or of the people who lived in it, the two cousins found a temptation from this period of walking thither almost every day. They called at various times of the morning, sometimes separately, sometimes together, and now and then accompanied by their aunt. It was plain to them all that Colonel Fitzwilliam came because he had pleasure in their society, a persuasion which of course recommended him still more; and Elizabeth was reminded by her own satisfaction in being with him, as well as by his evident admiration of her, of her former favourite George Wickham; and though, in comparing them, she saw there was less captivating softness in Colonel Fitzwilliam's manners, she believed he might have the best informed mind.

But why Mr. Darcy came so often to the Parsonage it was more difficult to understand. It could not be for society, as he frequently sat there ten minutes together without opening his lips; and when he did speak, it seemed the effect of necessity rather than of choice — a sacrifice to propriety, not a pleasure to himself. He seldom appeared really animated. Mrs. Collins knew not what to make of him. Colonel Fitzwilliam's occasionally laughing at his stupidity proved that he was generally different, which her own knowledge of him could not have told her; and as she would have liked to believe this change the effect of love, and the object of that love her friend Eliza, she set herself seriously to work to find it out. She watched him whenever they were at Rosings, and whenever he came to Hunsford; but without much success. He certainly looked at her friend a great deal, but the expression of that look was disputable. It was an earnest, steadfast gaze, but she often doubted whether there were much admiration in it, and sometimes it seemed nothing but absence of mind.

She had once or twice suggested to Elizabeth the possibility of his being partial to her, but Elizabeth always laughed at the idea; and Mrs. Collins did not think it right to press the subject, from the danger of raising expectations which might only end in disappointment; for in her opinion it admitted not of a doubt, that all her friend's dislike would vanish, if she could suppose him to be in her power.

In her kind schemes for Elizabeth she sometimes planned her marrying Colonel Fitzwilliam. He was beyond comparison the pleasantest man; he certainly admired her, and his situation in life was most eligible; but, to counterbalance these advantages, Mr. Darcy had considerable patronage in the church, and his cousin could have none at all.

CHAPTER XXXIII

MORE than once did Elizabeth, in her ramble within the park, unexpectedly meet Mr. Darcy. She felt all the perverseness of the mischance that should bring him where no one else was brought, and, to prevent its ever happening again, took care to inform him at first that it was a favourite haunt of hers. How it could occur a second time, therefore, was very odd! Yet it did, and even the third. It seemed like wilful ill-nature, or a voluntary penance, for on these occasions it was not merely a few formal inquiries and an awkward pause and then away, but he actually thought it necessary to turn back and walk with her. He never said a great deal, nor did she give herself the trouble of talking or of listening much; but it struck her in the course of their third *rencontre* that he was asking some odd unconnected questions—about her pleasure in being at Hunsford, her love of solitary walks, and her opinion of Mr. and Mrs. Collins's happiness; and that in speaking of

274

Rosings, and her not perfectly understanding the house, he seemed to expect that whenever she came into Kent again she would be staying *there* too. His words seemed to imply it. Could he have Colonel Fitzwilliam in his thoughts? She supposed, if he meant anything, he must mean an allusion to what might arise in that quarter. It distressed her a little, and she was quite glad to find herself at the gate in the pales opposite the Parsonage.

She was engaged one day as she walked in reperusing Jane's last letter, and dwelling on some passage which proved that Jane had not written in spirits, when, instead of being again surprised by Mr. Darcy, she saw, on looking up, that Colonel Fitzwilliam was meeting her. Putting away the letter immediately, and forcing a smile, she said—

'I did not know before that you ever walked this way.'

'I have been making the tour of the park,' he replied, 'as I generally do every year, and intend to close it with a call at the Parsonage. Are you going much farther?'

'No, I should have turned in a moment.'

And accordingly she did turn, and they walked towards the Parsonage together.

'Do you certainly leave Kent on Saturday?' said she.

275

'Yes—if Darcy does not put it off again. But I am at his disposal. He arranges the business just as he pleases.'

'And if not able to please himself in the arrangement, he has at least great pleasure in the power of choice. I do not know anybody who seems more to enjoy the power of doing what he likes than Mr. Darcy.'

'He likes to have his own way very well,' replied Colonel Fitzwilliam. 'But so we all do. It is only that he has better means of having it than many others, because he is rich, and many others are poor. I speak feelingly. A younger son, you know, must be inured to self-denial and dependence.'

'In my opinion, the younger son of an earl can know very little of either. Now, seriously, what have you ever known of self-denial and dependence? When have you been prevented by want of money from going wherever you chose, or procuring anything you had a fancy for?'

'These are home questions—and perhaps I cannot say that I have experienced many hardships of that nature. But in matters of greater weight, I may suffer from the want of money. Younger sons cannot marry where they like.'

'Unless where they like women of fortune, which I think they very often do.'

276

'Our habits of expense make us too dependent, and there are not many in my rank of life who can afford to marry without some attention to money.'

'Is this,' thought Elizabeth, 'meant for me?' and she coloured at the idea; but, recovering herself, said in a lively tone, 'And pray, what is the usual price of an earl's younger son? Unless the elder brother is very sickly, I suppose you would not ask above fifty thousand pounds.'

He answered her in the same style, and the subject dropped. To interrupt a silence which might make him fancy her affected with what had passed, she soon afterwards said—

'I imagine your cousin brought you down with him chiefly for the sake of having somebody at his disposal. I wonder he does not marry, to secure a lasting convenience of that kind. But perhaps his sister does as well for the present, and, as she is under his sole care, he may do what he likes with her.'

'No,' said Colonel Fitzwilliam, 'that is an advantage which he must divide with me. I am joined with him in the guardianship of Miss Darcy.'

'Are you indeed? And pray what sort of guardians do you make? Does your charge give you much trouble? Young ladies of her age are sometimes a little difficult to manage, and if she has the true Darcy spirit, she may like to have her own way.'

As she spoke she observed him looking at her earnestly ; and the manner in which he immediately asked her why she supposed Miss Darcy likely to give them any uneasiness, convinced her that she had somehow or other got pretty near the truth. She directly replied—

'You need not be frightened. I never heard any harm of her ; and I dare say she is one of the most tractable creatures in the world. She is a very great favourite with some ladies of my acquaintance—Mrs. Hurst and Miss Bingley. I think I have heard you say that you know them.'

'I know them a little. Their brother is a pleasant, gentlemanlike man—he is a great friend of Darcy's.'

'Oh! yes,' said Elizabeth dryly—'Mr. Darcy is uncommonly kind to Mr. Bingley, and takes a prodigious deal of care of him.'

'Care of him!—Yes, I really believe Darcy *does* take care of him in those points where he most wants care. From something that he told me in our journey hither, I have reason to think Bingley very much indebted to him. But I ought to beg his pardon, for I have no right to suppose that Bingley was the person meant. It was all conjecture.'

278

'What is it you mean?'

'It is a circumstance which Darcy, of course, could not wish to be generally known, because if it were to get round to the lady's family it would be an unpleasant thing.'

'You may depend upon my not mentioning it.'

'And remember that I have not much reason for supposing it to be Bingley. What he told me was merely this: that he congratulated himself on having lately saved a friend from the inconveniences of a most imprudent marriage, but without mentioning names or any other particulars, and I only suspected it to be Bingley from believing him the kind of young man to get into a scrape of that sort, and from knowing them to have been together the whole of last summer.'

'Did Mr. Darcy give you his reasons for this interference?'

'I understood that there were some very strong objections against the lady.'

'And what arts did he use to separate them?'

'He did not talk to me of his own arts,' said Fitzwilliam, smiling. 'He only told me what I have now told you.'

Elizabeth made no answer, and walked on, her heart swelling with indignation. After watching her a little, Fitzwilliam asked her why she was so thoughtful.

'I am thinking of what you have been telling me,' said she. 'Your cousin's conduct does not suit my feelings. Why was he to be the judge?'

'You are rather disposed to call his interference officious?'

'I do not see what right Mr. Darcy had to decide on the propriety of his friend's inclination, or why, upon his own judgment alone, he was to determine and direct in what manner that friend was to be happy. But,' she continued, recollecting herself, 'as we know none of the particulars, it is not fair to condemn him. It is not to be supposed that there was much affection in the case.'

'That is not an unnatural surmise,' said Fitzwilliam, 'but it is lessening the honour of my cousin's triumph very sadly.'

This was spoken jestingly; but it appeared to her so just a picture of Mr. Darcy, that she would not trust herself with an answer, and therefore, abruptly changing the conversation, talked on indifferent matters till they reached the Parsonage. There, shut into her own room, as soon as their visitor left them, she could think without interruption of all that she had heard. It was not to be supposed that any other people could be meant than those with whom she was connected. There could not exist in the world *two* men over whom Mr. Darcy could have such boundless influence. That he had been concerned in the measures taken to separate Mr. Bingley and Jane she had never doubted; but she had always attributed to Miss Bingley the principal design and arrangement of them. If his own vanity, however, did not mislead him, *he* was the cause, his pride and caprice were the cause, of all that Jane had suffered, and still continued to suffer. He had ruined for a while every hope of happiness for the most affectionate, generous heart in the world; and no one could say how lasting an evil he might have inflicted.

'There were some very strong objections against the lady,' were Colonel Fitzwilliam's words; and these strong objections probably were, her having one uncle who was a country attorney, and another who was in business in London.

'To Jane herself,' she exclaimed, 'there could be no possibility of objection; all loveliness and goodness as she is! her understanding excellent, her mind improved, and her manners captivating. Neither could anything be urged against my father, who, though with some peculiarities, has abilities which Mr. Darcy himself need not dis-

dain, and respectability which he will probably
never reach.' When she thought of her mother,
indeed, her confidence gave way a little; but
she would not allow that any objections *there*
had material weight with Mr. Darcy, whose
pride, she was convinced, would receive a deeper
wound from the want of importance in his
friend's connexions, than from their want of
sense; and she was quite decided at last that he
had been partly governed by this worst kind
of pride, and partly by the wish of retaining
Mr. Bingley for his sister.

The agitation and tears which the subject
occasioned brought on a headache; and it grew
so much worse towards the evening that, added
to her unwillingness to see Mr. Darcy, it determined her not to attend her cousins to Rosings,
where they were engaged to drink tea. Mrs.
Collins, seeing that she was really unwell, did
not press her to go, and as much as possible
prevented her husband from pressing her; but
Mr. Collins could not conceal his apprehension
of Lady Catherine's being rather displeased by
her staying at home.

CHAPTER XXXIV

WHEN they were gone, Elizabeth, as if intending to exasperate herself as much as possible against Mr. Darcy, chose for her employment the examination of all the letters which Jane had written to her since her being in Kent. They contained no actual complaint, nor was there any revival of past occurrences, or any communication of present suffering. But in all, and in almost every line of each, there was a want of that cheerfulness which had been used to characterise her style, and which, proceeding from the serenity of a mind at ease with itself and kindly disposed towards every one, had been scarcely ever clouded. Elizabeth noticed every sentence conveying the idea of uneasiness, with an attention which it had hardly received on the first perusal. Mr. Darcy's shameful boast of what misery he had been able to inflict gave her a keener sense of her sister's sufferings. It was some consolation to think that his visit to Rosings was to end on the day after the next, and a still greater, that in less than a fortnight

283

she should herself be with Jane again, and enabled to contribute to the recovery of her spirits by all that affection could do.

She could not think of Darcy's leaving Kent without remembering that his cousin was to go with him ; but Colonel Fitzwilliam had made it clear that he had no intentions at all, and agreeable as he was, she did not mean to be unhappy about him.

While settling this point, she was suddenly roused by the sound of the door-bell, and her spirits were a little fluttered by the idea of its being Colonel Fitzwilliam himself, who had once before called late in the evening, and might now come to inquire particularly after her. But this idea was soon banished, and her spirits were very differently affected, when, to her utter amazement, she saw Mr. Darcy walk into the room. In an hurried manner he immediately began an inquiry after her health, imputing his visit to a wish of hearing that she were better. She answered him with cold civility. He sat down for a few moments, and then getting up, walked about the room. Elizabeth was surprised, but said not a word. After a silence of several minutes, he came towards her in an agitated manner, and thus began—

'In vain have I struggled. It will not do. My feelings will not be repressed. You must

284

allow me to tell you how ardently I admire and love you.'

Elizabeth's astonishment was beyond expression. She stared, coloured, doubted, and was silent. This he considered sufficient encouragement; and the avowal of all that he felt, and had long felt for her, immediately followed. He spoke well; but there were feelings besides those of the heart to be detailed, and he was not more eloquent on the subject of tenderness than of pride. His sense of her inferiority—of its being a degradation — of the family obstacles which judgment had always opposed to inclination, were dwelt on with a warmth which seemed due to the consequence he was wounding, but was very unlikely to recommend his suit.

In spite of her deeply rooted dislike she could not be insensible to the compliment of such a man's affection, and though her intentions did not vary for an instant, she was at first sorry for the pain he was to receive; till, roused to resentment by his subsequent language, she lost all compassion in anger. She tried, however, to compose herself to answer him with patience, when he should have done. He concluded with representing to her the strength of that attachment which, in spite of all his endeavours, he had found impossible to conquer;

285

and with expressing his hope that it would now
be rewarded by her acceptance of his hand. As he
said this, she could easily see that he had no doubt
of a favourable answer. He *spoke* of apprehension and anxiety, but his countenance expressed
real security. Such a circumstance could only
exasperate farther, and, when he ceased, the
colour rose into her cheeks, and she said—

'In such cases as this, it is, I believe, the
established mode to express a sense of obligation
for the sentiments avowed, however unequally
they may be returned. It is natural that obligation should be felt, and if I could *feel* gratitude,
I would now thank you. But I cannot—I have
never desired your good opinion, and you have
certainly bestowed it most unwillingly. I am
sorry to have occasioned pain to any one. It
has been most unconsciously done, however, and
I hope will be of short duration. The feelings
which, you tell me, have long prevented the
acknowledgment of your regard, can have little
difficulty in overcoming it after this explanation.'

Mr. Darcy, who was leaning against the
mantelpiece with his eyes fixed on her face,
seemed to catch her words with no less resentment than surprise. His complexion became
pale with anger, and the disturbance of his mind
was visible in every feature. He was struggling

for the appearance of composure, and would not
open his lips till he believed himself to have
attained it. The pause was to Elizabeth's feelings dreadful. At length, in a voice of forced
calmness, he said—

'And this is all the reply which I am to have
the honour of expecting! I might, perhaps,
wish to be informed why, with so little *endeavour*
at civility, I am thus rejected. But it is of small
importance.'

'I might as well inquire,' replied she, 'why,
with so evident a design of offending and insult-
ing me, you chose to tell me that you liked me
against your will, against your reason, and even
against your character? Was not this some
excuse for incivility, if I *was* uncivil? But I
have other provocations. You know I have.
Had not my own feelings decided against you
—had they been indifferent, or had they even
been favourable, do you think that any consideration would tempt me to accept the man
who has been the means of ruining, perhaps
for ever, the happiness of a most beloved
sister?'

As she pronounced these words Mr. Darcy
changed colour; but the emotion was short, and
he listened without attempting to interrupt her
while she continued—

'I have every reason in the world to think ill

of you. No motive can excuse the unjust and ungenerous part you acted *there.* You dare not, you cannot deny that you have been the principal, if not the only means of dividing them from each other—of exposing one to the censure of the world for caprice and instability, the other to its derision for disappointed hopes, and involving them both in misery of the acutest kind.'

She paused, and saw with no slight indignation that he was listening with an air which proved him wholly unmoved by any feeling of remorse. He even looked at her with a smile of affected incredulity.

'Can you deny that you have done it?' she repeated.

With assumed tranquillity he then replied, 'I have no wish of denying that I did everything in my power to separate my friend from your sister, or that I rejoice in my success. Towards *him* I have been kinder than towards myself.'

Elizabeth disdained the appearance of noticing this civil reflection, but its meaning did not escape, nor was it likely to conciliate her.

'But it is not merely this affair,' she continued, 'on which my dislike is founded. Long before it had taken place my opinion of you was decided. Your character was unfolded in the recital which I received many months ago from

Mr. Wickham. On this subject, what can you have to say? In what imaginary act of friendship can you here defend yourself? or under what misrepresentation can you here impose upon others?'

'You take an eager interest in that gentleman's concerns,' said Darcy, in a less tranquil tone, and with a heightened colour.

'Who that knows what his misfortunes have been, can help feeling an interest in him?'

'His misfortunes!' repeated Darcy contemptuously; 'yes, his misfortunes have been great indeed.'

'And of your infliction,' cried Elizabeth with energy. 'You have reduced him to his present state of poverty—comparative poverty. You have withheld the advantages which you must know to have been designed for him. You have deprived the best years of his life of that independence which was no less his due than his desert. You have done all this! and yet you can treat the mention of his misfortunes with contempt and ridicule.'

'And this,' cried Darcy, as he walked with quick steps across the room, 'is your opinion of me! This is the estimation in which you hold me! I thank you for explaining it so fully. My faults, according to this calculation, are heavy indeed! But perhaps,' added he, stopping in his walk, and turning towards her, 'these offences might have been overlooked, had not your pride been hurt by my honest confession of the scruples that had long prevented my forming any serious design. These bitter accusations might have been suppressed, had I, with greater policy, concealed my struggles, and flattered you into the belief of my being impelled by unqualified, unalloyed inclination ; by reason, by reflection, by everything. But disguise of every sort is my abhorrence. Nor am I ashamed of the feelings I related. They were natural and just. Could you expect me to rejoice in the inferiority of your connexions ?— to congratulate myself on the hope of relations, whose condition in life is so decidedly beneath my own ?'

Elizabeth felt herself growing more angry every moment ; yet she tried to the utmost to speak with composure when she said—

'You are mistaken, Mr. Darcy, if you suppose that the mode of your declaration affected me in any other way, than as it spared me the concern which I might have felt in refusing you, had you behaved in a more gentlemanlike manner.'

She saw him start at this, but he said nothing, and she continued—

'You could not have made me the offer of

your hand in any possible way that would have tempted me to accept it.'

Again his astonishment was obvious; and he looked at her with an expression of mingled incredulity and mortification. She went on—

'From the very beginning—from the first moment, I may almost say—of my acquaintance with you, your manners, impressing me with the fullest belief of your arrogance, your conceit, and your selfish disdain of the feelings of others, were such as to form that groundwork of disapprobation on which succeeding events have built so immovable a dislike; and I had not known you a month before I felt that you were the last man in the world whom I could ever be prevailed on to marry.'

'You have said quite enough, madam. I perfectly comprehend your feelings, and have now only to be ashamed of what my own have been. Forgive me for having taken up so much of your time, and accept my best wishes for your health and happiness.'

And with these words he hastily left the room, and Elizabeth heard him the next moment open the front door and quit the house.

The tumult of her mind was now painfully great. She knew not how to support herself, and from actual weakness sat down and cried for half an hour. Her astonishment, as she reflected on what had passed, was increased by every review of it. That she should receive an offer of marriage from Mr. Darcy! that he should have been in love with her for so many months!—so much in love as to wish to marry her in spite of all the objections which had made him prevent his friend's marrying her sister, and which must appear at least with equal force in his own case—was almost incredible!—it was gratifying to have inspired unconsciously so strong an affection. But his pride, his abominable pride—his shameless avowal of what he had done with respect to Jane—his unpardonable assurance in acknowledging, though he could not justify it, and the unfeeling manner in which he had mentioned Mr. Wickham, his cruelty towards whom he had not attempted to deny, soon overcame the pity which the consideration of his attachment had for a moment excited. She continued in very agitating reflections till the sound of Lady Catherine's carriage made her feel how unequal she was to encounter Charlotte's observation, and hurried her away to her room.

Printed by T. and A. CONSTABLE, Printers to Her Majesty
at the Edinburgh University Press

www.ingramcontent.com/pod-product-compliance
Lightning Source LLC
Chambersburg PA
CBHW020846020726
47497CB00005B/1271